HALF MOON

Larry Alexander

trated by Phyllis Emmert

phyllisemmert.com

Published in the United States by IngramSpark

ISBN: 979-8-218-29350-5

Printed in the United States of America

Introduction

As I've gotten older I will sometimes wake up at about 3:00 a.m. Then I can't get back to sleep for an hour or two. I think this happens to a lot of people my age. After a few early mornings of lying in bed thinking about nothing, I decided to get proactive. So twelve years ago I began writing a book in my mind during these nocturnal awakenings. Not just any book though. This is my theory about UFOs: their origin, their habitat, and why they are here.

Growing up in the 1950's and 1960's, there wasn't much conversation about UFOs and flying saucers. But there were events. On June 24, 1947, Kenneth Arnold was flying his CallAir A-2 airplane by Mt. Rainer when he witnessed nine disc-shaped objects flying in formation. He said they looked like "a saucer if you skip it across water." Then there was the Roswell incident. Mac Brazel found unusual debris scattered on his ranch in mid-June, 1947. Only until Brazel learned of the flying disc craze taking place around the United States did he bring some of the material he had found to the local sheriff. The sheriff in turn contacted the U.S. Army. At first the U.S. Army said it was a flying saucer that had crashed during a thunder storm. Then the next day Lt. Col. Jesse Marcel showed the press shiny pliable material and said it was from a weather balloon. The story died.

But the flying disc craze did not. Concerned about mass hysteria concerning flying saucers in the late 40's, the Truman Administration began Project Sign, a systematic study of UFO reports. It was conducted by the U.S. Air Force. In 1952, the name was changed to Project Bluebook. It was terminated in 1969.

In the early 50's there was George Adamski flying with ETs in their ships to various planets. He wrote three books about his adventures. One of them was <u>Flying Saucers Have Landed</u>. As a kid, I owned a copy. In the late 50's out in the Mojave Desert by Giant Rock in Landers, CA, George Van Tassel was conducting UFO conventions on his property. He also claimed to have ridden in UFOs and received divine counsel from "Solgonda." Van Tassel built the impressive

Integratron a few miles away.

Betty and Barney Hill were one of the first ET abductions that took place on September 19, 1961. A book, TV appearances, and a movie followed. I even remember seeing Barney Hill on the TV show, "To Tell the Truth."

Then something happened in 1978 that changed the UFO conversation landscape forever. During an interview, Lt. Col. Jesse Marcel, retired, said the weather balloon had been a cover story to divert attention. He believed the Roswell debris was extra-terrestrial. Chris and I visited Roswell several years ago. We spent time at the International UFO Museum and Research Center, dedicated to providing information about the Roswell Incident. We drove to the flying saucer crash site and got as close as we could. But the biggest pleasant surprise was Dr. Robert Goddard's laboratory at the Roswell Museum. Considered one of the founders of modern rocketry, he moved to Roswell in 1930 and continued his research there.

Much has been written about UFOs during my years of sleepless early mornings. After disclosures by the U.S. government and the Air Force, there seems to be a renewed interest in this phenomenon. Politicians have talked more about UFOs. There have been several movies made depicting ETs in all sorts of ways. The TV show, "Ancient Aliens," shows intriguing and compelling evidence that UFOs and flying saucers may have been around our planet for a long, long time.

So if UFOs, flying saucers, and ETs are considered real, where do they come from? Proxima Centauri is the closest star to the sun with a planet orbiting it that is theorized to be in the "habitable zone." It is just over four light years away. Supposing you could crank up a ship to travel the speed of light, that would be an eight-year round-trip. Wouldn't it be easier just to be here somewhere without all the travel?

Another part of my theory has to do with the moon. The moon is big. It is the largest natural satellite relative to the size of the planet it orbits. It is the fifth largest moon in the Solar System. It rotates once every 27.3 days, meaning one side of the moon is always facing earth.

I know that astrophysicists can explain this phenomenon talking about the moon being tidally locked in a synchronized orbit about the earth, but it seems odd to me. And does anybody remember this photo

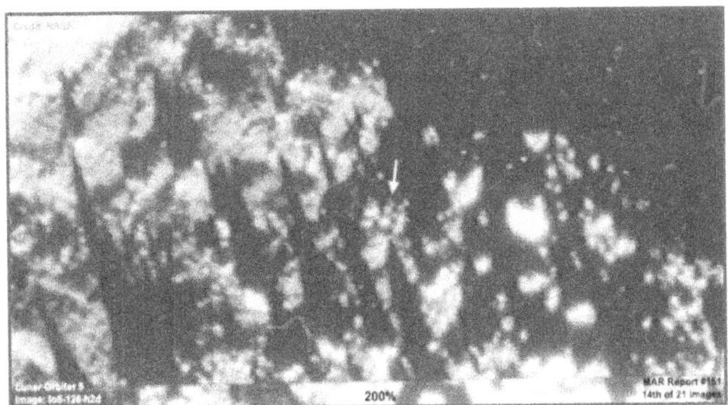

taken by Moon Orbiter 5? It was 1967 or 1968 and it appeared on the front page of the Everett Herald. The photo shows several spires on the moon's surface. I cut it out and saved the photo for a long time. No explanation of the spires was ever forth coming and the story disappeared.

It's a different world now from when I was ten years old talking to my dad about flying saucers. No such thing, he'd say, forget about it.

Well, anyway, people ask me all the time if there is going to be a sequel to Half Moon. (No one has ever asked me). If anyone actually did ask, the answer would be no. I'm so tired of making crap up.

HALF MOON

1

Self-Abduction

The Sixth Kind

It was an early Tuesday morning in March when I woke up and noticed a strange light coming from outside the master bathroom's window. It was pale green and pulsating. My wife, Kate, was awake, too, and saw the green light. "Mike, what is that?" she asked.

"Don't know," I said. "I'll take a look." As I got up I noticed the clock on the night stand. It was 2:33 a.m. At least it wasn't 3:33 a.m.

I opened the bedroom door and walked down the hallway to the foyer. Coming through the windows, the pulsating light caste an eerie greenish glow in the house. As I looked around, I saw the number 188,843 suspended above the table in the foyer. It, too, was pulsating. Wow, that's weird. What the hell is going on here? Well, one thing at a time. Where's this green light coming from? I walked over to the front door. On tip-toes, I looked out the front door window.

At first glance, it looked like three children wearing sunglasses petting our dogs. Floating about eight feet above the kids was a green glowing doughnut-shaped object. The doughnut was about ten feet in diameter and flat. Well, there was the source of the pulsating light, whatever that thing was. Now, what were the neighbor kids doing in my yard at 2:30 in the morning?

I looked back down at them. Something wasn't quite right here. First of all, the kids weren't wearing sunglasses. They were big, almond-shaped, black eyes framed in large heads with narrow, small chins. Next, the arms and fingers were way too long. It didn't look like there were enough fingers, either. And, they weren't wearing any clothes. As I'm trying to make sense of what I'm seeing, the kids' heads slowly turned to look right at me.

Well, I didn't feel comfortable inviting them into our home yet, so I turned on the porch light, opened the front door and walked

outside. It wasn't quite flight or fight, but I thought I had better be proactive. As the dogs came over to get petted I asked, "Hey, uh, what are you guys up to this morning?"

I wasn't prepared for what happened next. A huge, sharp, piercing pain hit the front of my forehead. It was excruciating and spread to the back of my eyes. "Ohhhh!" I yelled as I fell to my knees holding my head with both hands. I bent over with my forehead in the grass. I found it difficult to breathe. I tried to open my eyes. I couldn't. Even the pale light of the porch lights blinded my eyes. The intense pain began to move from behind my eyes to the middle of my head. My breathing was labored. Now, the back of my head began experiencing this intense pain. Very slowly, the pain began to subside. I tried opening my teary eyes again. With difficulty, I looked at the ground directly in front of me and saw three blurry pairs of three-toed feet. I lifted my head slightly and examined each creature. They all seemed to be exactly the same. They were about four feet tall. Their skin was a light grey color with no hair anywhere. They had no nose to speak of and a small horizontal indentation where the mouth should be. Their skin was covered with small bumps, like that of some reptiles. But there were small subtle differences, too. The one on my left had bigger skin bumps than the other two. The one directly in front of me had some kind of red mottling on the left side of its face, like rosacea. And the one on my right, no kidding, its' head was shaped just like that of Louie Armstrong's, a.k.a. Satchmo.

I slowly got up on my knees. There seemed to be nothing threatening about them at the moment. Were all three trying to answer my question at once and overloaded my frontal lobes? "Okay," I said, "From now on, one at a time answering me, please." Pointing to the one with rosacea, I asked, "How about you, Rosie, what are you here for?"

~Refueling our craft, ~ came the answer.

Now, that was strange, I thought. Even though Rosie didn't say anything, it communicated with me. It didn't happen as individual words in my mind, but as a whole thought. I felt exactly what it was thinking. It was like getting a mental snapshot.

"So, where is your craft?" I asked. They looked at one another, and then the one with the big lumps pointed straight up.

Directly above me was the flat, green doughnut, but now with the help of the porch lights providing some contrast, I finally saw an outside edge about thirty feet from the doughnut, forming a circular ship. The way the edge curved away from the doughnut, I estimated that the height of the middle of the ship was about ten feet as it tapered out to its edge. The color was exactly like its surroundings, dark and dull looking, making it virtually impossible to see.

"Hey, wait a minute," I said, "What do I have in my yard that you use as fuel?"

Once again they looked at one another, and then the thought came from Satchmo. ~Deer.~

Deer, an organic fuel?! What a concept! The damn things eat your plants, flowers, shrubs, and gardens—not to mention running into them with your vehicles from time to time. ~We only take ill and old deer. They don't seem to mind,~ thought Rosie.

"Please, take all you want," I said. They started moving under the doughnut. With some difficulty, I rose to my feet.

"Is the refueling complete?" I asked.

~We are ready to resume our observations.~

The ship slowly descended to where they were standing. I had to bend over to avoid hitting my head on the bottom of their ship. One by one, I watched Rosie, Satchmo, and the one with big lumps reach their hands into the doughnut. Their bodies were slowly being pulled up into the ship. All of a sudden, this idea hits me and I blurted out, "Hey, any chance I could take a joy ride with you all?"

~Reach into the craft,~ thought Rosie. Well, okay. And if things don't stay on a friendly basis inside their ship, I might be able to handle the three of them.

I reached my hands up into the darkness of the doughnut, evidently the door of their ship, and began being drawn in. As I entered the inside of their ship the sensation was a soothing warmth and relaxation. I was stunned by how great it felt, and exclaimed, "Jesus!"

~We took him on a joy ride, too.~

I was entirely inside their ship. How do I describe this? It seemed to be filled with a warm, viscous liquid, like Jell-O before it solidifies. Or better yet, the ship was like an individual cell and I was inside as an organelle in the cytoplasm. It literally felt like I was a part of their ship. I could feel and see in all directions. Inside the ship, it was like there was no outside of the ship. I then realized I wasn't breathing, even though my heart was pounding. I must be getting oxygen somehow. And, I discovered, there was another. I probably couldn't handle four of them.

Trying to keep things on a friendly basis, I said to it, ~Greetings, what are you up to?~

~I am operating the craft.~

Wait a minute, I must have thought my question. I certainly can't open my mouth and talk in this stuff that surrounds me. And James T there heard me and responded. Well, that was something.

The ship began to lift and move forward. As we accelerated, there was no sensation of movement. Newton's Three Laws of Motion didn't seem to operate in here. As we climbed, I looked around for controls and instruments, but couldn't see any. Nor could I tell how the ship was being powered. How did they make this thing go?

~Gravitational electro-magnetism,~ thought Satchmo. ~One day you will use gravity instead of opposing it.~

~How do you command the craft to maneuver?~ I thought.

~We use different signals from inside ourselves and direct them through the craft's medium.~ Rosie responded. That was interesting.

Suddenly, without warning, we went into a vertical dive. We were heading right towards a stand of evergreen trees. Once again, there was no sensation of a free-fall, but the trees and ground were fast approaching. Was something wrong with their ship? Was I being tested in some way? Were we going to crash, like at Roswell? This time, not only would there be extra-terrestrial bodies, but a human one as well. How would the U.S. Army explain that one?

At tree-top level, we pulled out of our dive. Just as we started to climb again, I heard this god-awful blood-curdling howl that scared the crap out of me. What the hell was that?

~Sasquatch,~ Satchmo thought, ~We occasionally frighten them.~

My god, they just buzzed Big Foot. And I was getting a distinct feeling of humor and fun from them.

~We have a relationship with Sasquatch.~

We climbed once again and headed west at a highly accelerated rate. I noticed the front of the ship began to elongate forward and the side walls began to close in, as did the overhead and deck. Evidently, this was making the ship more aerodynamic. Even though it was a moon-lit night, I could see out of the ship like it was daytime. We cleared the Cascade Mountains heading to Puget Sound. We flew over Whidbey Island, Edmonds, Elliott Bay and suddenly stopped, hovering over the Seattle Seahawks' Lumen Field. ~A familiar landmark for you,~ thought Rosie.

~How long did it take us to get here, Rosie?~

~Approximately 240 earth seconds.~

So let's see, a quick calculation; 240 seconds equals 4 minutes, it's roughly 250 miles from Tonasket to Seattle, so dividing 250 by 4 is about 60 miles per minute. Okay, one last calculation; 60 miles times 60 minutes equals 3,600 miles per hour. How did they do that?

~God almighty!~ I thought.

~Can you explain that phrase?~ asked Rosie.

~Not really,~ I thought, ~I'm just astounded at how fast we travelled here.~

~It is time to return you to your origin,~ Rosie thought.

~Guys,~ I thought, ~As a kid, I always dreamed of being an astronaut and travelling in space. Any chance on our way back we could spend a few seconds in outer space? I may never get another chance like this again.~

They looked at one another. I could feel their consultation about my request. It seemed they wanted to accommodate me on a limited level when finally James T turned to me, and asked,

~Will going to the fourth planet suffice?~

Going to Mars? I can't believe it! ~I'm in!~ I exclaimed

~In what?~

~Yes, the fourth planet will suffice.~

The ship rotated vertically 90 degrees and we shot out of Seattle heading straight up. I couldn't believe I was actually headed to Mars. How long was this going to take? In all the excitement I forgot about Kate back in Tonasket. This could potentially take days, or weeks. I began to have a bad feeling about this decision. Just when I was going to voice my concerns, Rosie thought, ~Do not be concerned.~

I thought, ~Okay, I'm trusting you to get me back to my origin soon.~

~What is trusting?~

~Mmm, I will explain later.~

The clouds disappeared and I saw stars and galaxies in the black vastness of outer space. I started to get this tingly feeling throughout my body, kind of like getting goose bumps when you're cold. Was the medium in the ship getting colder the more we travelled into space?

~We are approaching light velocity. The sensation you feel will dissipate,~ thought Rosie.

~You're going to Mars at the speed of light?~ I asked , incredulously.

~No, we cannot travel at the speed of light. We will accelerate to, in your terms, approximately 250,000 kilometers per second.~

~How do you accomplish this?~ I asked.

~Neutrinos.~ was Rosie's answer.

I watched the moon whiz by. Were those dwellings I saw on the far side? As the moon disappeared behind us, I looked forward into the vast blackness of space. I thought to myself, this is hard to comprehend.

~A wise statement,~ thought Rosie. ~Focus on the pale red point of light in front of us.~ As I did, the pale red point slowly became larger and larger. Finally, the surface features were becoming recognizable. Mars.

The ship began to slow down and finally stopped. Mars was right there in front of us: huge, brilliant, astounding, humbling. There was Olympus Mons and the three shield volcanoes to the west. One of the shield volcanoes was partially covered in clouds. Looking to the east, like a huge open tear in the middle of the planet was Valle Marinais, the largest canyon in the solar system. I just stared at the ruddy red planet completely overwhelmed. I could feel reverence from my fellow travelers, too. Soon though, it was replaced with a little impatience. I turned to them and simply thought, ~Thanks.~ Immediately, we turned around and headed back to earth.

As I lowered out of their ship, our dogs, Bill and Sammie, came over and began licking my legs. I moved back from the center of the ship's door as Rosie, Lumpy, and Satchmo came down. I shook their hands, three fingers each, and I guess a thumb, thinking, ~That was pretty cool, guys.~ They looked at one another and I sensed confusion. ~Thank you so much,~ I thought. ~This has been one of the best experiences I have ever had!~

~You are surprisingly reasonable and patient,~ Rosie thought.

~Will you come back here again?~

~Yes.~

~Soon?~

~Very soon. Fare well.~

After they boarded, the ship shot straight up in the morning sky. At about a thousand feet it stopped like it was hesitating, then came back down across the other side of the valley and strafed an aspen grove. That horrible howling sound filled the morning air. My god, were there Sasquatch that close to our home? The ship then went straight up and out of sight. I stood there looking up at the morning sky, full of stars and wonder. Finally, I looked down and petted the dogs. I walked over and opened the front door. Before I shut off the porch lights, I noticed a picture on the table in the foyer. It was of me and our two boys at a Seahawks football game. We were wearing Seahawks jerseys with the numbers 18, 88, and 43 on them. Well, the last of the morning's mysteries was solved. I walked down the hallway to our bedroom, and quietly opened and closed the bedroom door. I crawled back in bed, exhausted. Kate was asleep. I looked at the clock on the night stand. It was 3:34 a.m.

It has been about six weeks now since that night. The ETs hadn't come back, at least as far as I know. ~Very soon~ could mean fifty years, who knows. Maybe they get thirty million miles per deer and refueling won't take place for a long time. I kept going out into the front yard looking for something that they might have left behind, like other-worldly excrement or forgotten tools. Maybe I should have gotten their autographs. Oh, well. You know, maybe it was just a dream. Yeah, maybe it was a dream. It was a pretty damn cool one, though.

Tonight Kate has taken me to the local Mexican restaurant for my birthday dinner. After we ordered our food, she handed me a present. "What's this?" I asked.

"Oh, some little thing I thought you might enjoy."

I unwrapped the gift. It was a framed photograph with a somewhat dark, greenish background. As I studied the picture, the images became clearer. I'm asking myself, what's some naked guy doing with three small children and two dogs? I glanced up at Kate with a questioning look, then stared at the photo some more until finally I said, "Oh, wow!"

There I am, nude, with Rosie, Lumpy and Satchmo. I completely forgot I didn't have any clothes on. I looked up from the picture at Kate.

"Have a nice flight?" she asked with a knowing smile.

As my grin widened, I answered, "I did."

2

Crystal Green Persuasion

Golf's a goofy game. Take the other day. I met with the usual guys, Ray and Ted, for eighteen holes of golf. We play a points game that we created, the loser having to buy Coronas for everyone at the 19th-hole. Even though it's only a beer, the game can get tense and hard-fought with lots of laughs along the way.

Today, we are playing a new course that Ray has recommended. The first tee is quite elevated. Using the railroad tie steps, we reached the top to find four 6th grade students ready to tee off. They saw there were only three of us and said we could go ahead of them. The first hole was a challenge. There was a wooded slope on the right side with three-foot high fescue growing on the hillside. The left side had the clubhouse almost sticking out into the fairway.

We've all rented clubs and I noticed Ted's bag was made of clear plastic filled with gasoline. I just thought, wow, that's got to be heavy packing that around. Ray's clubs seemed fine. My clubs however, were all two-feet long, except for the three-wood. It seemed about the right length.

We teed off. Miraculously, all of our drives found the fairway. On the way down the steps, Ray told us the only way to the first fairway was through the pro shop. So we made our way through the pro shop door, then entered a room filled with golf equipment and apparel. The room was huge and seemed to extend in all directions forever. As I'm about to go through the door that has a sign reading TO FIRST FAIRWAY, I realized that I didn't have my golf clubs. Where did I put them? I began looking on clothing shelves and countertops for the rentals. Did I lean them up against a table? I walked down a couple of aisles with no luck. This could take forever. Standing next to the 40%-off rack, I felt a tapping on my shoulder. I turned around to see who it was. It was Rosie standing there with my golf clubs.

What the heck was Rosie doing in the clothing section of the pro shop with my clubs? Rosie kept tapping my shoulder. Suddenly, I began to feel my body slowly float upward. It's like I'm underwater returning to the surface. I began to feel the water pressure diminishing and the surroundings getting brighter. As I broke through the surface of my subconscious, I opened my eyes. In our moonlit bedroom, I looked up from my bed to see three pairs of large, black, almond-shaped eyes staring at me. Rosie was still tapping my shoulder.

I bolted upright and yelled, "Ahhhhhhhhhhh!" Kate woke up and said excitedly, "What's the matter!?"

With my heart pounding, I said "Nothing, nothing. It's just a leg cramp. Sorry." I thought, ~Jeez, Rosie, what are you guys doing here?~

~We seek your assistance.~

~Guys, it's like 3:00 a.m. You scared the crap out of me. What's going on?~

Silence. They just stood there looking at me. I've got to get them out of the bedroom before Kate gets a look at them. I don't even want to think about what the ensuing scene would be like. I got out of bed and said to Kate, "I've got to walk this leg cramp off. I'll be back in a minute. Go back to sleep."

I walked to the bedroom door as Rosie, Lumpy, and Satchmo followed. As I opened the door, I noticed that it was still locked. We always locked our bedroom door from the inside at night. How did these guys get in? As they proceeded through the doorway, Rosie thought, ~To the craft.~ We marched down the hallway to the foyer. I opened the front door which was also still locked. How are they doing that? I directed them outside and thought, ~I'll be along in a minute~.

Once I came out, we headed for their ship hovering in its usual spot just above the front lawn and sidewalk. We all petted Bill and Sammie along the way and one by one, entered the ship. I had forgotten how great it felt to be inside their ship. Whatever the medium was around me, it was warm, soothing, and I don't feel one ache or pain. It seemed to help calm my mood after the rude awakening. No wonder James T stays inside the ship while the others venture outside. ~James T, nice to see you again. How are you doing?~

~Acceptable.~

~Where are we off to this morning?~ I asked

~Off to?~ responded James T.

Let's see, how do I want to think this? ~Where are we on to this morning?~

~A ceremony of a spiritual nature.~

That sounded interesting. ~What's our heading? No, wait, which direction are we going?~ I asked

~Circular~.

All right, I'm done trying to make small talk; just sit back, relax, and enjoy the flight.

Kate woke up and felt for Mike in bed. He wasn't there. She decided maybe he needed help with his cramp and got up to find him. Kate walked down the hallway, through the foyer, past the living room and into the kitchen, turning lights on as she went; no Mike. Then she saw the note on the kitchen counter.

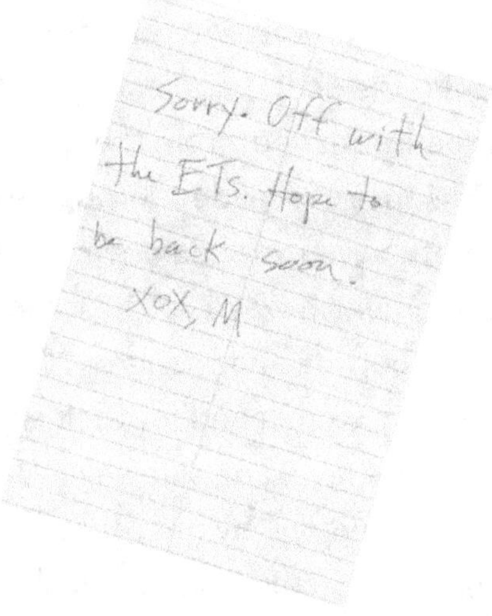
Sorry. Off with
the ETs. Hope to
be back soon.
XOX, M

As the ship climbed and accelerated, our heading appeared to be east. As before, there was no sensation of motion, and the outside surroundings appeared to be in daylight. But instead of skimming tree tops and mountains, like the Seattle trip, we climbed above the clouds to the upper reaches of the atmosphere. As we headed to our destination, wherever that was, blue is turning black and I began to see the curvature of the earth before me. It was an awe-inspiring sight. It looked like a huge blue and white marble hanging in space with the bluish shimmer of the atmosphere on the horizon. As I stared at this celestial wonder before me, I noticed that colors were beginning to change. The blue and white were being washed out and the corona of the atmosphere was becoming brighter. Then suddenly, the sun appeared temporarily blinding me. The ship dampened the sun's blinding light and I could once again look eastward.

After a while, I noticed no one was thinking anything, so I thought, ~Hey Rosie, since our last encounter, what have you all been up to?~

~Observing,~ was the answer.

~So what assistance do you need from me?~ I asked.

Rosie thought, ~You first need to observe the spiritual ceremony.~

Lumpy turned towards me and asked, ~How long have you been with the other human?~ Trying to answer scientifically, I thought, ~Forty orbits of the closest star.~

~Is that substantial?~

~Well, it's pretty good for being with the same person, compared to a lot of other people.~

~And you have reproduced two times?~

~Yes, we have two boys.~ This seemed sort of personal from the guys, but at least we were making small talk. I thought, ~And how about you, anyone special in your life?~ No response. I decided to let it go.

Soon, we began our descent. The sky was slightly overcast with scattered clouds as we came down by a small coastal town. Most of the buildings were white as they clung to the cliffs and steep banks above the sea. It was dark blue with patches of turquoise. The day was beautiful with sunbreaks accenting the town. We came to a stop and hovered at an altitude of about a thousand feet. By the looks of it, we were in the Mediterranean somewhere.

~Observe downward,~ thought Rosie. I looked down at my feet (jeez, nude again) when the ground seemed to come straight up to the ship. Somehow, the bottom of the ship was magnifying what was directly below it. We were observing a wedding in progress. It was taking place in an open-air ornate stone courtyard surrounded by small balconies covered in ivy that hung down. The priest, in flowing white robes, was standing before the bride and groom as they were exchanging vows. The groom was dressed in a black tuxedo and the bride was wearing a white lace wedding dress with a long train. The dress had a low-cut front, and from my vantage point, revealed ample cleavage. Dressed in various colors, the onlookers were making it all look quite festive. The ET's timing was impeccable.

Off to the side was a stone stairway with wrought iron railings leading up to an outdoor dining area overlooking the sea. There were several round tables with white linen table cloths and napkins folded to resemble local sea birds. Every table setting had white china, assorted glass and silverware, with floral center pieces. There was a detailed tile mosaic in the center of the floor. There was a lattice-work of white crossbeams supported by white stone columns over the entire dining area. I hated to think of how many lyres this was costing someone.

~What is the significance of this spiritual ceremony? ~asked Satchmo.

~Well, it's a religious bond between a man and a woman that says, in front of God, they will live together harmoniously and abide by the vows that they have stated during the ceremony,~ I answered.

~What is God?~ asked Lumpy. Oh, they weren't throwing softballs anymore.

I thought, ~I'm no expert, but most people of the earth believe in a deity or Supreme Being of some sort that usually promises eternal life for living an abiding and peaceful life. You know, it's something or someone to have faith in.~

~What is faith and do you have to possess it to reproduce~? asked Lumpy. What were these guys driving at? ~No, Lumpy, you don't have to have faith to reproduce,~ I responded. I felt the guys' mood shift from hope to disappointment. They no longer seemed interested in the wedding, but still remained confused about God and faith. I needed visual aids of some sort to help with my explanation. Then it hits me.

~Let me take you somewhere that might be more helpful in explaining this.~ I could sense a meeting of their minds, when finally James T asks, ~Where is this destination?~

~Let's head to the Seattle Seahawk's stadium. Once there, I will show you where to go.~

After we arrived in Seattle, I directed James T to the south end of Whidbey Island and the small town of Clinton. This was where I grew up. And this was where there was a small church with an even smaller congregation; built in 1911, it was St. Peter's Lutheran Church. The ship came down and hovered just above the gravel parking lot next to the back of the church.

~We need to go inside so I can try to explain a few things,~ I thought. One by one, the four of us descended from the ship onto the ground. Once outside, I remembered that even during the late spring, Whidbey's marine air can be rather brisk, and I have no clothes on. This was going to be a quick lesson. Between the church and the graveyard was a small path that took us to the side door at the back of the church. I am hoping the key was still in its usual spot. Leading up to the door were three steps with a wood railing. On the last step, the railing leveled out with a small piece of wood about the size of a candy bar on it. I lifted the piece of wood and after 42 years since I had been here last, the key was still underneath the piece of wood. I unlocked the door and turned around to direct the guys into the church. They were standing there exchanging glances at one another. After a few seconds Lumpy thought, ~One day we will show you a better way of securing entrance into a structure.~

Walking through the small kitchen, we entered the Sunday School room. Wow, this is the place where I used to sing "This Little

Light of Mine" and memorized and recited the 23rd Psalm so I could earn a free bible; Standard revised version. Off to the left were the stairs leading to the inner sanctum of the church itself. After climbing the stairs and walking through the doorway, we were all inside standing close to the altar. I found the light switches. With a couple tries, the sanctuary was illuminated.

Scanning the inside of the church, not much had changed. The high steeple above the narthex housed the bell that was rung by pulling on a rope. The rope still hung through a hole in the ceiling by a post. The nave had high ceilings with the usual ornate podiums and lecterns. In the sanctuary was the altar and behind the altar was a large painting depicting Jesus Christ just after the resurrection. He was standing dressed in robes of various colors showing his wounds to Thomas. I looked at the bare-chested Jesus. I had always thought his nipples were too close together in the painting. Oh, well.

~Ok, guys, most people who believe in God may come to a building like this one to worship. They try to follow God's rules, and hopefully, God will choose them to be with Him throughout eternity. Not everyone makes it. If you don't believe in God or follow his rules, you supposedly burn forever in a place called hell.~ I hope I'm not diminishing my chances of a trip to heaven with this explanation.

~What is the purpose of this?~ asked Rosie pointing at the altar.

~This is the altar. Notice how it surrounds the shrine. It has a little padded step in front of it so people can kneel and pray and pay tribute to God~.

~Is this God?~ asked Lumpy, looking at the painting of Jesus Christ.

How do I explain this one? I'm not sure I know myself? ~This is Jesus Christ, God's son,~ I thought. ~ But then, God is also Jesus Christ and somewhere you throw in the Holy Ghost. It's called the trinity.~ I was getting a feeling of confusion, and a sense of anxiety from the guys. As a former teacher, you can always tell when you're losing your students, and this was one of those moments. In desperation, I said out loud, "Guys, this is the Supreme Being, this is the Creator!"

All of a sudden my head felt like it is going to split in two. As before when I first met the ETs, I dropped to my knees holding my head. The pain was excruciating. It wasn't letting up, but getting worse. As tears came to my eyes, I began to sense surprise and excitement from Rosie, Lumpy, and Satchmo. Looking at one another, they gestured wildly with their arms and hands. Soon, they began to notice me on the floor and the pain started to ease up. With difficulty, I thought, ~I'm not kneeling and praying before God, guys. Please stop with all the excited communication!~ I slowly looked up and Rosie is standing right in front of me. He walked around to my back, took hold of my shoulders, and began lifting me to my feet. This guy was strong. Was this Judas with the final act of betrayal?

Rosie turned me around. Facing one another, he excitedly thought, ~Creator! You thought Creator! Now we have something to show you!~

Their ship slowly lowered down to my driveway. As I descended from it, I was still reeling from what I had seen, heard, and felt. Rosie, Lumpy, and Satchmo joined me on the driveway. Light-headed and unsteady on my feet, I tried to regain my balance. I thought, ~Guys, I appreciate your faith in me, no pun intended. I hope I was of some assistance in your concern.~

Rosie responded, ~You appear to be moonstruck, no pun intended.~

Did Rosie actually come up with a joke? I began to laugh when I noticed the little slit on Rosie's face, the one that kind of looked like a mouth. It appeared that the corners of the slit were going up. Was Rosie trying to smile? ~Your assistance has helped us understand many things about ourselves and gives us a new resolve in our mission,~ Rosie commented.

~Well listen, don't be strangers. I look forward to seeing you soon.~

~We did not think we were strangers, and you will see us soon,~ thought Rosie. With that, we shook hands and they ascended into their ship. I watched as they shot straight up into the morning sky and disappeared. Man, what a night. I felt cold, wet noses on my legs. I bent over to pet Bill and Sammie. "There's something you don't see every day," I said to the dogs, "A joke-cracking ET." I stood up, turned to walk to the front door and saw Kate standing in the doorway. Mmmmm...

"Do you think this is such a good idea?" she asked.

"Probably not, maybe, I don't know. I just experienced something I'm having trouble sorting out in my head."

"Come inside. It looks like its cold out," she says with a somewhat wry smile. I look downed. "Nice", I said.

We went inside. While I got my bathrobe on, Kate made us each a cup of tea; no earl grey for me, thanks. As we sat down in the living room, she asked, "Where did you go this time?"

"Oh, Italy, I think, and Clinton, and the moon." Kate just stared at me. "They're clones of some sort, you know. They can't reproduce."

"Is that a problem?" she asks.

"Well, they've been around, I guess, for thousands or millions of years, maybe more. And through accidents and crashes, like the one at Roswell, their numbers have diminished," I explained. "They need to find replacements to continue their mission here on earth, whatever that mission is."

"Can't they make more of themselves?" she asked. "How many of them are there?"

"That was the whole point this morning. No, they can't," I shrugged. "They don't have the knowledge. Isn't that interesting? I have no idea how many of them there are. I've only seen these four ETs." I took a sip of the tea. I'm not a tea person, but it tasted pretty good.

“Here’s my take on this whole thing. Once the ETs realized their population was diminishing, they began to try to figure out how to make more of themselves. They started looking for answers. They knew that humans can reproduce, so they began doing some up-close and personal exams. You’ve heard of alien abductions taking place in the 50’s and 60’s. Most people claiming to have been abducted report being examined sexually, one way or another. Some of them even developed genital warts. Who knows why?”

Kate asked, “Are these the same ETs you’ve been hanging out with?”

“Maybe, but listen. It all kind of makes sense. Remember the cow mutilations? Some big cattle ranches here in the West had found cows surgically operated on, usually involving the reproductive organs. No one ever figured out how someone could mutilate a cow with laser precision. One theory was ETs. If it were ETs, examining humans and taking cows apart didn’t help their problem. I think, eventually, they noticed a link between religion, marriage and reproduction. Wondering if this was a possibility, they decided to do some research. Hence, my adventure this morning.”

“They can fly near the speed of light, but lack knowledge to reproduce. That seems weird to me,” Kate says.

“Well, listen to the rest of my story and maybe it will make more sense.”

I began telling Kate about my morning with the guys, or gals, or maybe they’re something in-between. I described the Italian wedding and the strange questions Rosie, Lumpy, and Satchmo kept asking; like can you reproduce if you have a church wedding and what is God? I told her I thought a few visual aids would help my religion lecture, so I took them to St. Peter’s Church in Clinton. It was there, I explained, that we had our big breakthrough, even though it damn near killed me, again. It was the fact that I called God the Creator that got the ETs excited. Rosie said they now had something to show me, and off to the moon we went.

"So what does going to the moon have to do with religion and reproduction?" Kate asks.

"Keep listening," and I began telling her about my trip to the moon.

As the ship flew around the far side of the moon, we went into a steep dive towards one of the large craters. We weren't slowing down and the closer we got to the moon's surface, the more anxious I became. ~Guys, I've had too many heart-stopping adventures today. I really don't want another.~ No response. I closed my eyes waiting for the crash. Nothing. When I opened them, it appeared we were descending through a large tunnel. ~Crap, guys, quit doing that stuff to me!~ Silence. Finally, we reached an opening that led into a huge circular chamber. It had a tall, dome-shaped ceiling and a floor that curved away from where we were hovering. I could not see the other side. My god, it looked like half the moon was hollowed out. I was trying to take all this in when I saw Rosie pointing towards the center of the underground chamber. In the distance was a pale, greenish glow. It appeared to be several miles away.

We slowly proceeded to the green glow, eerily similar to my first encounter with the guys in our front yard. Soon, I began to see the tops of several objects. The closer we got, the more these objects seemed to be growing right out of the floor. I guessed it was the curvature of the ground that gave this illusion. The large objects began looking like a humongous agave' plant. A few moments later, I could finally make out what they were; huge, green crystals. They were the size of some of the tallest skyscrapers on earth, maybe taller. The crystals were six-sided, some straight up and down, and some tilted. There appeared to be hundreds of them coming right out of the moon's floor in the colossal chamber. It looked like they covered about a twenty-acre circle. Surrounding the crystals on the ground was an odd looking wall; about four feet high, dark grey in color resembling concrete.

It was very jagged and extremely uneven. The wall was so close to the crystals that some of them hung over the wall. About a hundred yards from the wall, the ship stopped. The guys started getting out, even James T. Rosie communicated that they wanted me to join them. I asked Rosie if I was going to be safe outside the ship. Rosie explained that it was the same medium inside this huge underground cavern as it was inside their craft. Well, okay. So, out I went. Surprisingly, it was exactly the same. The only difference was 1/6 gravity. The guys began a sort of hop-walk towards the crystals with me in the rear. About ten feet from the wall, they stopped. Rosie turned to me and thought, ~This is *our* altar.~

Standing in front of the crystals, I asked, ~Is this the Creator?~

~This is the Creation put here by the Creator,~ thought Rosie. ~This is our purpose in being.~

Looking at the huge crystals, the soft green light seemed to shimmer inside, as if it was a liquid of some kind. I couldn't tell if the green light was coming from below ground or if the crystals produced the light themselves. It was bright enough to read by. For some reason, I had a sudden impulse to touch one of the crystals.

~You may touch the Creation, ~ thought Rosie. ~We may not.~ I looked at the guys as if to get some reassurance, and Rosie's head nodded at me. I walked over to the dark, grey wall and slowly raised my arm towards the closest crystal. I extended my fingers. Was something going to happen when I touched it? Was I going to get an electrical shock or something worse? My hand began shaking when my fingers were only an inch away. I forced my hand to get closer. Finally, my index and middle finger made contact. The crystal was warm to the touch. I started to lower my arm making a slow stroke downward with my entire hand on the crystal's surface. Suddenly, like a balloon filling up with too much air and exploding, my mind began receiving a stream of information: events, dates, people. I could not process it all and evidently, I passed out. The next thing I knew, I was in their ship heading back to earth.

"Are you okay?" asked Kate sympathetically.

"Just a little groggy getting out of the ship. I feel fine now," I said.

"So how did you find out about the ETs being clones and not being able to reproduce?" asked Kate. "And the crashes and Roswell?"

"By touching the Crystal. And there's so much more, but I'm having trouble understanding any of it."

"So when did the ETs finally figure out they were clones?" asked Kate.

"I'm guessing, but I think the Crystals must have given me information about the ETs that they found useful. I'm sure they read my thoughts after my encounter with the Crystals," I explained. "You can't keep too many secrets from them inside their ship."

Kate thought for a moment. "I don't know, but I think they're using you for something."

"Well, you might be right, but for some reason I trust them," I said. "And the feeling I get from the guys is that they trust me. And like

I said, I don't seem to have any ill-effects by my crystal encounter."

Kate turned, reached over and knocked on our wood coffee table.

The rest of the day passed by as usual. I drove to town and did a little shopping at the local hardware store. We grilled steaks with Brussel sprouts for dinner that evening. After dinner we watched a Seattle Mariners game that we had recorded. Kate and I were in bed and asleep by 10:30 p.m. That night, I didn't dream about golf or ETs. I dreamt about how the pyramids were built, what happened to the Mayans, where Amelia Earhart is, and who shot J.F.K.

3

The Truth is Out There, Really

This was the worst hang-over I've ever had and I didn't even drink any alcohol. I had a splitting headache. You know, the kind that settles in right behind your eyes. And my right shin was throbbing. Kate and I were staying at a bed and breakfast in the Green Lake area of Seattle. It was 8:30 a.m. and raining hard. I'm sitting on an old leather couch in the living area with my Ray-Bans on. There were several ornate throw rugs on an old hard-wood floor, the kind that squeaks with every footstep. One wall had a library built around an old player piano. Across from me were curtained windows looking out to huge Douglas fir trees and beyond that, Green Lake. Off to the right of the windows was the front door being opened by a young couple with umbrellas, evidently off to do some early sight-seeing and maybe some shopping. The cool, fresh air from the open door was soothing to my face.

Standing next to me was an older gentleman trying to make small talk. I just nodded or shook my head to his endless observations and questions. He was with the woman this morning at breakfast who never stopped talking, seemingly even when she was chewing and swallowing. Now, it appeared he was making up for his silence when his wife was not around. "Did you know," he said, "that if the Seattle Center Monorail needed parts replaced, they had to be custom made because the original German contractor that built the Monorail was long out of business?"

He had this horse shoe haircut going on with about eight grey strands on the top of his head combed straight back. His rather large belly was tucked into his pants. Later in life, that's one thing most men must decide; was their belly going to hang over the front of their pants, or were they going to tuck their belly into their pants? He had chosen the latter. And to round it out, he was a change jingler; you know, a pocket full of about $10 worth of coins that he kept rolling over with his hand in his pants pocket. Jeez.

Finally he said, "Well young man, you have a nice day," and slapped the back of my shoulder as he left. The pain in my head was excruciating.

On my left was the staircase leading up to the four guest bedrooms on the second floor. A couple with their toddler were coming down. They made their way through the open double-doors to the dining room. They found a table and immediately the boy pulls his chair out, snags a throw rug tipping the chair over onto the hardwood floor. The crashing sound made me wince with pain.

Kids. As good parents, they will try to prove you wrong most of the time. It's eventually getting to that position in life when parenting either smooths out or sort of disappears. Of course, your kids had to be at least in their 30's for this transition to take place. That's where Kate and I found ourselves now. One of the pleasant perks we've discovered being parents of older children was traveling to all the places they had lived or were currently living. Travis, our oldest at 37, had been pretty adventurous. Starting in Olympia, Washington, at The Evergreen State College he had lived in Toronto, London, Washington D. C., and now resides in Bermuda. Our other son Joel, 33, had been fairly domestic staying in-state. He had lived in Bellingham to Lake City to Northgate and now Green Lake. As a preschooler Joel was into drawing, particularly whales: orcas, humpbacks, narwhals, blue whales, sperm whales, and belugas. He said he was going to be a marine biologist studying orcas in the San Juan Islands north of Seattle. However, childhood dreams become reality with changing views. He is currently a project manager for Sound Transit working on expanding the light-rail system. So, we were here visiting with him for a couple of days.

Kate and I have rented a room at the Green Lake Bed and Breakfast, an older stately two-story home across the street from Green Lake. Painted in steel-blue with a light brown trim, it featured a front porch supported by four pillars with two dormers above. Upon entering, we met briefly with the owner to learn about the house amenities and rules. With bags in hand, we went up the creaky wooden staircase in search of our room. When we reached the landing upstairs, I noticed the hallway was rather long with a short set of steps at the other end leading up to a door. Were they going up to another room or just the attic? Before I had a chance to look we arrived at our room, The Lakeside. We opened the room door and I walked over to the curtained windows and looked out. We weren't by the lake nor could you see the lake through the huge fir trees across the street. Oh, well.

That evening Kate and I took Joel out to dinner at the Green Lake Bar and Grill, a great little restaurant and bar. After dinner, we made arrangements to meet in the morning for a shopping and eating trip in downtown Seattle. Only five blocks from the bed and breakfast, Kate and I walked back and thank God, it wasn't raining. As we entered the living room of the bed and breakfast an elderly couple was sitting in front of the fireplace reading their books. We exchanged hellos and goodnights as we went up the stairway to our room. Curiosity got the best of me and I climbed the stairs at the end of the hall. I tried the door. It was unlocked. I slowly opened it to see a small porch. This one did not have a roof. Well, not as interesting as I had imagined.

After a nightcap in the room, we crawled into bed. I made a mental note of the room's layout. It's become a habit of mine when in a strange room to see the best path to the bathroom when there's no light. We fell asleep to the sound of rain; not outside, but from an electronic device on the nightstand. It featured the recorded sounds of ocean waves, babbling brooks, song birds, and rain.

Around 3:30 a.m., according to the babbling brook machine, I woke up needing to go to the bathroom. The pressurized sensation was unrelenting. As I got out of bed, I mentally charted my path to the bathroom. The door was open with a little nightlight by the bathroom sink. The toilet was directly ahead of me with the tub and shower to my right. I shut the door, lifted the lid and began relieving myself. Out of the corner of my eye, I noticed the shower curtain slowly opening. What the hell? Now the curtain has my full attention. What was going on? The curtain continues to slide, eventually revealing Rosie, Satchmo, and Lumpy standing in the tub. I momentarily gasped and

fell back, urinating all over the tile work behind and under the toilet. ~Greetings,~ thought Rosie. ~We want to show you something of interest.~

"Good god almighty! What the hell are you doing?" I yelled. Son of a bitch! Can't I have an evening uninterrupted by these guys? Trying to calm myself, I asked ~Is there a reason I had the sensation to urinate so badly?~ No Answer. ~Close the curtain so I can finish in private.~

Followed by the guys, I came out of the bathroom. I whispered, "Oh Kate..." Before I could finish, "Be back by 7:00 a.m. for breakfast," she says, "and be safe!" Being prudent this time, I walked over and gave her a kiss. "Don't worry. I'm not very happy with them right now."

As I turned to go with the guys, I thought, ~I'm getting dressed this time. It's colder than hell outside.~

Lumpy thought, ~Only organic material is allowed in the craft.~

"What!?" I exclaimed.

~We thought you knew.~ thought Satchmo. Thinking back, I was nude getting out of bed both times joining them. I sighed, ~Lead the way.~

Leaving our room, I looked both ways making sure no one was wandering the hallways. Maybe the ETs were taking care of that for me. I followed them up the short stairway at the end of the hall and onto the small porch. The weather was brutal with wind, rain and temperatures at a cool 44 degrees. What I wouldn't give for some non-organic material now?

Leaning against the wall was an old wooden ladder that led to the roof. We all climbed up as I saw the familiar green doughnut floating just above us. Once on the roof, I reached up and ascended into their ship. The warming sensation was miraculous, thank god.

~Hello James T, and if you must know, I'm not a very happy camper.~ James T flashed me a somewhat confused look, but I decided to ignore it. Let them figure it out for a change.

As their ship climbed away from Green Lake, it appeared we were headed in a westerly direction. I wondered what there was that would be of interest to me. I noted that our flight was being made in complete silence. Maybe they knew I was really upset with them. No, they knew. I doubt there's anything private around these guys.

We broke through the clouds. The night sky seemed more brilliant than usual. I busied myself by studying the cosmos. I don't know who it was that named the stars and constellations, probably the Greeks and Romans, but a lot of the names were so beautiful: Cassiopeia, Andromeda, Alpha Centauri, Aldebaran, Polaris, Aquarius, and many more. After quite some time of identifying constellations, we began a slow descent.

The skies were clear and moonlit. Looking down, I finally figured out that we were not over land, but water. It had to be the Pacific Ocean shimmering below. In the distance, I made out some lights that appeared to be on an island. Our rate of descent did not change as we approached the ocean. Oh shit, we're not slowing down. Before I could yell, we struck the water and continued our descent for another hundred feet or so. What is down here that's going to peak my interest? All of a sudden, we came alongside a humpback whale with her calf. My insides were about to explode from the very sight of being next to two whales. I can't stand the silence any longer. ~Rosie, is this what you wanted to show me?~

~Yes, but there is more.~

Jeez, what could that mean? ~More!? What does more mean?~

~We want you to go within the humpback whale with us,~ thought Rosie.

Holy crap! What is Rosie talking about? Actually going inside the whale? For what purpose? I've got to slow this whole thing down so I don't do something really stupid, like being late for breakfast.

~First, where within? And second, I'm not going.~

~To go within means to enter the whale's brain, its mind, by using our minds. We will experience the humpback whale's thoughts and feelings.~

~And how am I supposed to do this?~ I asked.

~You will follow us. Drop your eye lids,~ commanded Rosie. I did not drop my eye lids. They dropped anyway.

Through my mind's eye, I saw the guys. ~Do you see us?~ asked Rosie.

~Yes,~ I thought.

~Follow us,~ thought Rosie. We made our way through the ship, into the ocean, and towards the whale. As we approached, strands or ribbon-like waves began emanating from, I guess, where the whale's brain was located. The waves grew towards us. It was like rays of sunbeams shining through clouds. There were about seven of them. The ones in the middle were almost a translucent pink. The rest became redder the further out they were from the whale. The frequency of the waves also increased as they went out. It was quite beautiful and they all seemed to shimmer in the dark, blue water.

~Rosie, what am I seeing?~ I asked.

~These are pathways to within.~

~So this is how we get inside the whale's mind, hop on one of these?~

~Yes. We will board a pathway.~

~Which one are we taking?~ I asked.

~You can use anyone of your choosing. We can only travel on logical and mathematical pathways. Those are the ones in the middle with the least wave length and color.~

Mmmm. So I'm assuming the red and higher frequency pathways must be emotions like, love, hate, envy, jealousy and so forth. Would a whale be able to exhibit some of those emotions? Maybe I'll find out shortly.

I followed the guys on one of the pink translucent pathways. It was slowly taking us closer to the whale until it appeared we were being absorbed into it. Suddenly, it became very dark with a faint soft glow in the background. This was not what I expected to see. Where were the synapses and spider web-like nerve channels with electrical impulses firing off on these nerve highways of the brain? As if to answer my question, Satchmo thought, ~We are entering the mind of the humpback whale.~

Oh, the whale's mind, not the brain. I wondered what the difference was. And then, surprisingly, two things happened simultaneously. It became a little brighter, but the second thing was extraordinary. I was awash with pure thought, pure emotion from the whale. I recognized it was the mother's love for her calf. I felt warmed, soothed, and comforted. If you've ever had major surgery, it was like when the anesthesiologist administers the juice, the Valium stuff into your system; a warm rush that relaxes your entire body. This was how it now felt. I didn't want to leave. Ever.

I couldn't see the guys anymore, but I heard Rosie think, ~It is time to return to the craft.~ I didn't want to go. I didn't want to leave this blanket of warmth, love, and devotion; just awhile longer, please!

I felt a gentle nudging as the cooler surroundings outside the whale's mind began to envelope me. Following the guys, I was on the pink pathway back to their ship.

~Did we have to leave so soon?~ I asked. Like coming out of major surgery, I was groggy and trying to get my bearings back.

~You were in danger of not returning at all,~ thought Lumpy.

Oh, but what a way to go.

Rosie looked up at me and thought, ~We are offering an incentive for you to enter into an agreement with us.~

What!? It sounded like they wanted to make a deal of some sort with me. But to what end and what's the carrot they're evidently going to dangle? Maybe we were finally going to get to the crux of these nocturnal kidnappings. There's got to be a reason; talk about being apprehensive and curious at the same time. ~All right guys, what do you have in mind?~

I made it back to Green Lake for breakfast, Seattle shopping, and a well-deserved afternoon nap. This evening the real adventure was going to begin. I had to be well-rested and no alcohol allowed. Kate and I got to Joel's apartment at about 5 p.m. The weather was horrible, even for Seattle standards; 45 degrees, raining hard, with a strong southwest wind. The plan was to have happy hour before going to dinner at one of the local restaurants, except I wouldn't be accompanying them. I sat on Joel's couch when I mentally received the call.

"Hey, Joel. Want to see something?"

"Yeah, sure."

"We need to go up on the roof of the apartment building. You better bring an umbrella."

"What are you talking about?" asked Joel.

"Trust your father. Let's go."

Once outside Joel's apartment, we walked down the hallway and stepped outside to an open foyer. Immediately, the weather hit us; cold and wet. We followed the stairs to the roof, now exposed to all the elements. I saw that the ET's ship was directly overhead. I began looking forward to climbing into its warm confines. In a corner of the roof alongside a little wall was my old barbeque I had given Joel, sitting out in the rain. Nice. I instructed Joel to stay at the top of the stairs as I walked out to about the middle of the roof towards and under the green portal. (I thought I would start calling the doughnut something a little more technical; I don't think the guys got the metaphor anyway.) The rain was making a loud pounding sound on the tar paper roof.

"Hey," Joel shouted. "How come you're not getting wet?" I looked up and pointed. As he lifted his head upwards trying to understand what he was seeing, I turned around and began taking my clothes off. As I stepped out of my underwear, I yelled, "Please take my clothes in. Your mother will explain. Hope to see you in the morning before we head home."

I reached up into the green portal and was pulled into the ship. Ooh, it felt good inside. As the ship slowly began to turn and climb into the night sky, I looked down at Joel as his lips said, "What the f...!?" The guys and I were off to the moon.

Well, here was the deal, or part of it. I was going to enter the Crystals and seek an answer to any question of my choosing about earth's history. Evidently, the Crystals had the capacity to provide an inside look at anything that has taken place in earth's past. Who knew? I remembered what passed through my mind the first time I touched one of the crystals: dates, events, people...I just couldn't process the large stream of knowledge. Supposedly, now I can.

To explain: It took about twenty times with lots of help from the guys, but I finally learned how to create pathways and enter the humpback whale's mind. Now remember, I'm no genius so I could not have done this without them. And I don't even want to think about what they were doing with my head. Anyway, it goes something like this; close your eyes until you enter the negative visual world and then, the tricky part, give your mind a half to three-quarters twist that coincides with a twist of the whale's mind. Then, pathways will appear. Sounds kind of straightforward, but it was all about timing. And sometimes, it did take a lot of time.

So, we were on our way to the moon. I was going to attempt to enter the Crystals, have a historical question answered, and get out. Why they wanted me to go into the Crystals is beyond me. They were not saying their reason, yet. Once I do, then and only then will I learn what they will offer me, the incentive. Yeah, I know, I'm not much of a negotiator. But I'm curious as hell to find out what it was. I know what I want out of this deal.

As the moon was getting closer to us, I asked, ~It's alive, isn't it?~ All of the guys turned and looked at me for several seconds, maybe too long. Finally, Rosie thought, ~What is your subject of reference?~

~This ship,~ I thought, ~your craft, it's alive.~

~What is the basis of your statement?~ Rosie asked.

~Well, first of all,~ I began, ~there are no controls or instruments for operating or navigating your craft. Number two, James T never leaves the craft, except the time we went to the Crystals. I think he's like a cowboy riding his horse; this craft is his horse. Now, remember the first time we all met? Your craft was munching on old and sick deer. How would a machine digest a deer? Another thing, you can't bring anything onboard that isn't organic. I'm assuming it would be an irritant that could affect the ship's performance; like a piece of sand in an oyster. Speaking of marine animals, this thing behaves like some of them. It goes from 0 to 4,000 mph in no time, darts and dashes forwards, backwards, sideways, and up and down. Sometimes, it just sits and hovers. And, the first time I got into this thing, I thought it was like entering a huge single cell complete with cytoplasm or whatever this stuff is around us.~

~Let me go one step further; you guys are the organelles inside this single cell. Even though you venture out occasionally, you spend most of your time inside and I think there's a couple of reasons why. Each one of you has a special purpose inside here. It's like a symbiotic relationship with the ship somehow. And here's the other reason. I've never seen any of you ingest anything and I've certainly never seen anything come out because it appears to be physically impossible. So, you guys are like huge rechargeable batteries and this ship is your charger.~ They remained motionless.

~Well, how'd I do?~

Lumpy thought, ~We are here.~ I looked to the front of the ship and there was the Crystal Creation.

As we neared it, I could be wrong, it appeared to have grown a little since our last visit. As before, all the guys left the ship and walked towards it. About fifty feet from the first crystal, they stopped as I continued. When I got to arm's length of the crystal, I turned and looked at the guys. I heard a collective, ~Proceed.~

I looked at the green crystal and then looked up. It must be at least 300 feet tall. It glowed and shimmered. The inside of the crystal

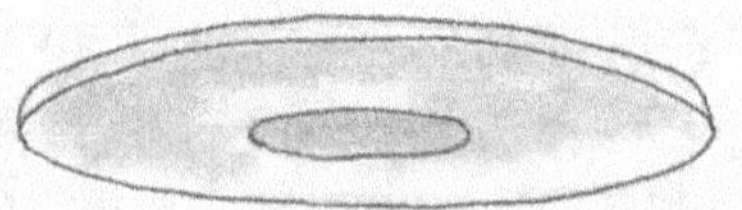

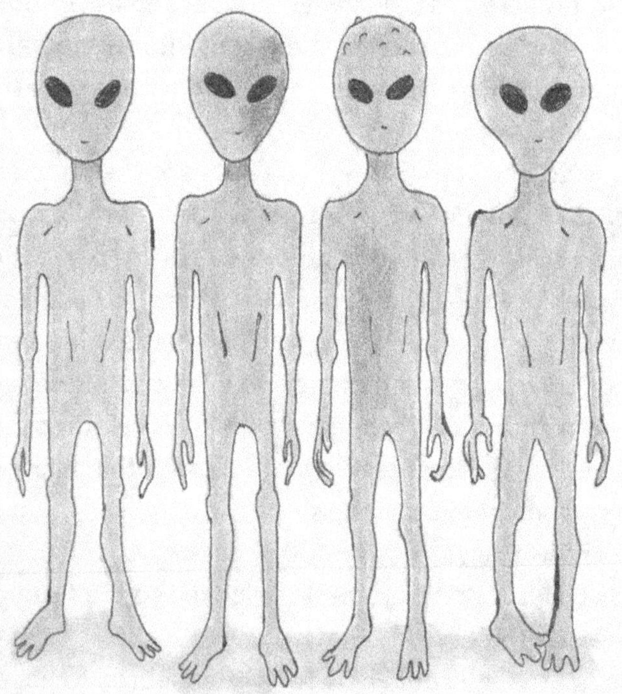

appeared to be moving underneath. You know, on your TV when you don't have a specific channel on and it's just a bunch of black and white dots moving around, that's what it looked like to me.
With a deep breath, I reached out to touch the crystal. My hand was shaking. As I laid my hand down on the crystal's side, I closed my eyes and found the negative world. With a mind twist, a single pathway appeared. It wasn't pink or red, or particularly wavy, just a grey slate color. With trepidation I hopped onboard with foreboding. This was not the same as entering the mind of the humpback whale. Wherever I was going seemed to be taking a very long time. The darkness was unsettling. What if I never get inside? What if I remain in some kind of flux never to return to the real world? As fear began to grip me, darkness became a faint light green until suddenly a diamond-shaped corridor came into focus. It appeared to stretch forever with no end in sight; a geometric wonderland of six-sided structures glowing with a green hue. On each side of the crystal lattice were hexagonal plates similar to a certain snow flake shape. The hexagonal plates were about the size of a cocktail napkin. Each side of the crystal lattice resembled the honeycomb of a bee hive.

On every plate was a scene of some sort: nature, buildings, people, animals, or combinations of all the above. One plate caught my eye. It was a castle with a purple and yellow flag flying in the breeze above it. As with the crystals on the outside of the Creation, the surface of the hexagonal plate appeared to shimmer and move. With my mind, I touched the plate and instantly was projected into the scene. I was literally standing next to the castle.

It was a hot summer day there with a beautiful blue sky above. However, about one hundred yards out surrounding the outside of the castle was a fog or mist. Something above me caught my eye. On the rampart stretching out between two towers was someone walking along the narrow pathway. He was a bearded young man wearing a type of guard uniform. There was a hood covering his head; a sort of woven wire mesh, maybe the original hoodie. He wore a purple and yellow tunic. The insignia on his chest was the same insignia that was on the flag. The tunic appeared to have metal shoulder pads with the same wire mesh as sleeves extending down to his hands. I stepped out of the castle wall shadow to get a better look when the guard looked down and saw me. Immediately, he yelled something and drew an arrow from his quiver. He loaded his crossbow and aimed it at me. I turned to run and tripped over a large stone as the arrow whistled passed my ear and struck the ground by my head. I pulled myself up and began hobbling towards the shimmering mist. I looked over my shoulder as two more guards were aiming crossbows at me. As I reached for the mist to get some cover, another arrow struck the ground just ahead of me. Then, as quickly as I had gotten into the castle scene, I was back in the diamond-shaped corridor. Was the mist a doorway back into the Crystals? Sweating, heart racing, and breathing heavily, I looked down at my throbbing shin to see blood trickling from a two-inch gash. This was not what I had expected; things were real and concrete in here. I've got to be more careful as I proceed.

For my quest of true knowledge I chose Stonehenge. Yeah, I know, I could have picked who killed JFK or which planet was Geraldo Rivera from, maybe at a later time. I had always been fascinated with the stone formation; how it was constructed, and really, what was its purpose? It seemed there's more that we don't know about Stonehenge than we do know. It is a prehistoric structure, but we don't know exactly when it was built, maybe 5,000 years ago. And who built it? Some say the Druids or it could have been the Romans. Maybe Merlin magically moved the twenty five-ton stones from Ireland to England. Some experts believe it was an astrological observatory, predicting eclipses and celestial events, such as the winter solstice. Others think it was a Druid temple or burial site, while some theorize it was a landing pad for extra-terrestrial space craft. Maybe I'll have to ask the guys if they know anything about that. It truly is one of the last unexplained structures on the planet. But how am I going to find Stonehenge among billions, if not trillions, of crystals? With all this conjecture and thinking about Stonehenge, the image of modern-day Stonehenge appeared in the crystal plate next to me. I didn't understand how it happened, but I wasn't arguing. I wanted to get out of here as soon as I could.

On a whim, I reached out and touched the left side of the crystal plate. Immediately, the crystal seemed to flip with a totally different look to the structure. It appeared newer. In fact, looking closely, it was complete; a circular structure with no missing rock slabs. It was breathtaking. Inside the large stone circle were smaller stones in a circular pattern. Inside that smaller circle were five large stone structures with three smaller stones in front of each. I touched the left side of the crystal plate again. Stonehenge was going back in time right in front my eyes. The image showed several workers measuring and aligning positions for the next stone slabs using primitive instruments resembling a sextant and a transit. Only four stone slabs were standing erect in a semi-circle. As I stood there mesmerized watching the crystal plate, a wave of nausea overwhelmed me and a feeling of foreboding, darkness, and doom. Either way, I suddenly did not feel well at all. This dark feeling was so strong that I was overwhelmed with the primitive emotion of fight or flight. I've got to get out of here I told myself, and fast. With one last shot at getting at least one question about Stonehenge answered, I touched the right side of the crystal plate several times to move Stonehenge ahead in time. As it slowly moved forward in the crystal plate, Stonehenge's real purpose presented itself. I gasped and shouted, "Oh, my god!" Its original purpose hadn't even been used yet!

With the knowledge of this horrifying revelation, I lost my balance and stumbled backwards. I reached out with my right hand to brace my fall. It landed squarely on the crystal plate behind me. Immediately, I fell backwards hitting the back of my head on some type of floor. Barely conscious, I opened my eyes to see stars; not stars from a concussion, but real stars in a night sky. I laid there for a while watching them trying to regain full consciousness. I didn't recognize any of the star patterns or see familiar constellations. And then another wave of nausea hit me, but this one was different. The floor I landed on was moving. I suddenly felt seasick. I turned my head to see the floor I landed on was the wooden deck of a ship.

Struggling, I propped my body up on my elbows. Looking around, I had landed on the bow of what looked like a sampan. I saw two masts with riggings and polygon-shaped sails with the familiar horizontal ribbing. There was a cabin towards the bow with lights on inside. Fishing nets were neatly stowed by the stern. There was only one problem; the mist, my doorway back to the Crystals appeared to move along with the sailing ship. If I was to get back, I would have to jump into the water and swim for the mist; not my favorite choice. As I began to try to solve this problem, the answer appeared before me; a large dog with snarling teeth and a low, threatening growl. The growl became menacing barks as it approached. I then heard excited voices inside the sampan's cabin, getting louder. Looking for the nearest exit off of the fishing boat, I jumped up and ran, making a one-handed leap over the railing. I heard the snap of the dog's jaws close to my backside. I hit the water and began swimming as fast as I could to the mist. Come on, come on mist, get me out of here! Then, there I was laying soaking wet on the floor of the diamond-shaped corridor.

I gave a huge sigh of relief. Now I've got to get out of here. I struggled to get on my feet. My head was throbbing, my leg aching, and this dark foreboding, this feeling of doom was overwhelming me again. I felt sick to my stomach. Staggering to the end of the hall I tried to put my hand on the wall. It was shaking even worse than before. I closed my eyes and saw the grey pathway and attempted to get on. As I advanced, the pathway seemed to move away from me. I tried again, but the pathway remained out of reach. I was not making any progress. In fact, it felt as if something was pulling me backwards. Something has got a hold of me and was pulling me back.

~Guys! Guys!~ I thought excitedly. ~I'm not going to make it! There's something vile, wretched, and means to put an end to my existence!~ I could feel my mind letting go. I'm just not mentally strong enough to battle this phantom and get out of the Crystals at the same time.

All right, I told myself, give it one last chance, one last shot. I concentrated on the pathway. With all my mind and all my being, I began crawling towards it. My thoughts were positive and resolute. I kept moving and moving. The pale green light faded into darkness. I felt the pathway with my mind. As soon as I climbed on, whatever was trying to drag me back into the Crystals and destroy me, let go. My eyes opened to see the outside of the Crystals. I collapsed and fell to the moon's floor.

Kate walked up to me and said, "I've checked us out of here. Are you okay to be travelling?" I looked up and quietly said, "You're driving." With some effort, I stood up. I grabbed our bags as Kate held the door open and we walked across the street to our SUV. It was raining. As I set the bags down to open the lift gate, a woman walking on the sidewalk holding an umbrella stopped and said, "You're not getting wet."

I looked over at her. "What!?" Again, she said, "You're not getting wet." I looked at my coat sleeves. She was right. I was not getting wet even though it was raining. As I gazed up into the cloudy skies, I saw the pale green portal hovering several feet above me. As I did, my headache went away. I reached down and pulled up my pant leg; no wound, no scar. How do they do that? Their ship slowly climbed and disappeared into the clouds. I put the bags in the back of the SUV and shut the lift gate.

"Kate, I'll drive. Let's go home." I turned and saw the woman with the umbrella looking up mouthing, "What the f...!?"

4

Within Without

"Michael! Michael! Michael!"

Downstairs in the wine room, I was checking the acid level of our new batch of wine. We had just crushed 400 pounds of pinot noir grapes yesterday. The berries were juicy, very ripe, and sweet. The pinot noir color was a deep ruby red and the nose was already overwhelming. So far this was promising to be a very good wine. The brix was 26.3 which means the pinot noir should develop into a wine with lots of fruit notes. At least that's what I'm hoping for. That's what I always hope for with each batch of wine.

What was that? I straightened up and held still, listening.

"Michael! Michaellllllllllll!"

Kate! I dashed out the downstairs door on a dead run to the barn. Kate mentioned at morning coffee she was going to groom Babe, her horse, for a morning ride. What has got her all worked up, a rattlesnake, a bear, a cougar, or a skunk? Jeez, I hope it's either a rattlesnake, bear, or cougar.

I rounded the corner of the barn where the tack shack and hitching rail were. There's no Babe at the hitching rail. I looked to my right under the lean-to where the stacked bales of hay were. There was Kate, looking frantic. She was standing and pointing at the end of the hay stack. I slowly walked over to have a look-see, not knowing what to expect. Around the corner of the hay pile sitting on the dirt floor were Rosie, Lumpy, and Satchmo. They were playing with four of our kittens. Rosie looked up at me and thought, ~Has a problem occurred?~ I turned to Kate and she gives me a look that says, what are they doing here and what are you going to do about it?!

~What are you guys up to this morning?~ I asked.

~At our last meeting you presented your proposal as part of our agreement. This proposal requires that we interact with your biological partner. She has never met us. We asked you what behavior we should display here at your dwelling when we meet her.

We wanted your partner to be accepting of us. After several examples, you explained that she enjoyed the company of young felines. Since our part of the arrangement is transporting your partner to the country of Norway, we thought a proper introduction involving a mutual common attraction, such as these felines, was in order,~ explained Rosie.

~Are you here to pay off your part of the bargain~? I asked

~Pay off? No. We are here to complete our agreement. We will be here at 4:00 a.m., your time, tomorrow morning,~ thought Rosie.

Losing patience, Kate asked, “Aren't you going to say anything to them?”

“Trust me, I am,” I responded. I got the questioning eyebrow look. “Dear, (no, don't say that. She might end up in the belly of their ship) I mean Kate, let me introduce you to my friends.” Each clutching a kitten, Rosie, Lumpy, and Satchmo stood up. “This is Rosie, here is Lumpy, and lastly, Satchmo. Guys, this is my partner and wife, Kate.” After a troubling ten seconds of silence, Kate gives a weak, “Hi.” Rosie extended its' hand and reluctantly Kate gave a weak handshake. In turn, the rest shook hands with Kate. After another troubling ten seconds of silence, Kate asked, “How come they're not saying anything?”

“Once again, trust me, they are. They don't verbalize like we do, but use visions in the mind to communicate. If you're around them long enough, you'll catch on.”

Rosie thought, ~We must leave. We will return at the designated time.~ And with that, they put the kittens down, turned around and walked to the other side of the barn to board their ship.

“Why were they here, Mike?” asked Kate. Ah, the moment I've been waiting for, or dreading. “I made a deal with them. Remember, they wanted me to try and access the Crystals in the moon. I said I would try if they would help me with something,” I explained.

“So what did they agree to do for you?” Kate asked accusatorily.

“Well, you know how we've travelled to Scotland, Ireland, and England? Mainly, because this is my heritage on my father's side. Plus, they have lots of golf courses and pubs. And you know how I really don't want to go to Norway or Sweden like you do, even though it's your family heritage and half of mine on my mother's side. Anyway, to sort of make up for this I've arranged a lunch in Bergen, Norway, with your cousin Anna. You will begin the journey tomorrow morning at 4:00 a.m., arriving in Bergen a little before lunch time. You'll have lunch with Anna at a cute little eatery on Kaigaten Street."

It doesn't take long for the implications to sink in. "I am not flying with four strange beings from who knows where in their flying saucer anywhere. Not to mention I would be naked," Kate firmly exclaims.

"Okay, humor me for a second."

"I'm not humoring you or anyone else. The answer is no!" I thought, I have my work cut out for me. I could use a little other-worldly persuasion about now.

"Look, I think I've got the naked part worked out. When the ETs and I flew out of Green Lake, Lumpy said only organic material could be inside their ship. So, find an all-cotton dress and all-leather sandals and I think you'll be fine," I rationalized. Kate hesitated for a moment, a good sign.

"You've been in contact with Anna?" Kate asked.

"Yes, I have. With a day's notice, like now, she will meet you for lunch and give you a brief tour of downtown Bergen."

"And what time do I leave and how long is the flight?"

"The guys will be back at 4:00 a.m. tomorrow morning to pick you up. The flight will be about an hour. They will drop you off at Byparken Park. From there, it's a short walk down Kaigaten Street to Bergen Brunsj, the restaurant. You'll have about four hours until the ETs return to the park to bring you home," I said.

A silent thoughtful moment goes by, and finally, "Yeah, and they're playing with the kittens didn't hurt. Is a bag of peanuts included on this flight?" she asked. A little smile forms on my face and a little nod of my head.

The next morning 4:00 a.m. came and went without a hitch. Kate was wearing an old cotton print summer dress with leather sandals. I didn't ask if she had any underwear on. She reached her arms up into their ship. The green glow of the portal through the summer dress revealed the outline of Kate's body. She was still in excellent shape. As she ascended her expression was, I can't believe this, I'll get even, and what am I doing!? The ship didn't spit her out, so I guess her clothes were fine. And off into the morning sky they went.

It was a beautiful June morning on Pine Creek Road. The stars were brilliant, not a breath of wind, and the warm air inviting. I decided to have a cup of coffee on the patio and watch the sunrise come over the hills out of the east. I didn't do either.

I sat down on the chaise lounge and set my coffee cup on the small table next to it. I closed my eyes and began to think about each time I had been with the ETs. The first time I invited myself on their ship. Or did I? Maybe subconsciously I was being invited. The second time they presented their problem to me. There had been a few crashes of their crafts with crew members lost. They needed to figure out how to reproduce to keep their population steady and their mission ongoing. You'd think they would have planned for this eventuality. And exactly what was the ETs mission? All I've ever heard them think was "observing." And the third occasion I learned how to enter into the minds of living things and the Crystals. This was when we entered into the first part of an agreement; after I entered the Crystals I could answer any question I might have concerning any part of human history. Then I could ask a favor of them. So I requested they take Kate to Norway. No problem. Now that I review the agreement, it sounds like a win-win for me. Except, this is only the first part. I don't yet know what will be next.

So are they influencing me with some kind of mind meld stuff? Probably, and to what end I don't know. They still haven't solved their reproduction issue. If I'm involved in helping with this problem, what can I do? Is another trip to the Crystals on the agenda? I hope not. It now seems to me the mysteries in human history should be left alone, especially Stonehenge. Leave things a mystery so humans can contemplate about and try to solve them.

I adjusted my seating in the lounge chair, started to think about all the implications of solving the mysteries of human history through the Crystals when I nodded off.

Little did Mike know that in the ET's almost infinite wisdom, they were not aware of one of human beings' unique qualities. And by the evening, he and Kate would be fighting for their very existence.

The craft hovered above Byparken, a beautiful park in downtown Bergen. As the walking traffic dispersed, the craft made a sharp descent in between four deciduous trees by Christies gate. The portal came to rest on the grass lawn. Kate was instructed to stand on the grass. As she did the ship slowly ascended leaving Kate looking at Lille Lundegardsvann, a small lake in the middle of the park. She was amazed at how well she had travelled considering all the circumstances.

It was a brisk day in Bergen with broken clouds and some sun breaks. The park was beginning to show signs of summer with the deciduous trees leafing out and various flowers blooming with vibrant colors. Outlined with surrounding mountains, the park was stunning. Even though Kate only wore a summer dress, she didn't seem to mind while taking in the views. She made her way across the plaza and took a right on the angled walkway to Kaigaten Street. From there it was a short block to Bergen Brunsj Café.

The café was a two-story building with a small steeple above the restaurant. It was painted a brilliant white with Kelley green trim. The name, Bergen Brunsj, was above the entrance door which was framed by two large plate-glass windows. As Kate walked around the sandwich board advertising the day's specials, she saw Anna sitting at a table by one of the front windows. The last time she saw Anna was about ten years ago at her parent's home in Mukilteo, Washington. They were similar in age and stature; each possessing a spirited and lively personality. Kate walked through the door. Anna looked to see who had come through the entrance and saw Kate. Anna stood up and rushed over to where Kate was. Hugs and kisses were shared as they settled into the enjoyment of a family reunion and an exquisite lunch; champagne, scones and jam, small assorted sandwiches, fresh fruit and delicious chocolate pastries.

Anna eventually brought up the subject of Kate being in Bergen and how Mike was so flexible about their lunch time together, considering air travel, hotel reservations and ground transportation. Kate simply said, "Anna, suffice it to say that Mike can accomplish extraordinary things and this is one of them. So let's just enjoy our time together this afternoon." And Anna said, "Ya, let's do just that."

After lunch, Anna took Kate on a walking tour of downtown Bergen. After a little shopping and volumes of family history being discussed, it was time for Kate and Anna to say goodbye. With promises of lunches together in the future, Kate made her way back to the four deciduous trees in Byparken for her rendezvous with the ETs. After a short time waiting for foot traffic to clear, she entered the ship and was on her way home to Pine Creek.

Everything was as before. Rosie, Lumpy, Satchmo, and James T looked forward in their craft and seemingly thought of nothing. But Kate began to notice that the closer they were to her home, the more agitated they became. They would look at one another and then look forward. They all took small steps when they exchanged glances, and even James T, who normally concentrated on navigation, was also excitable. It became so apparent that Kate was becoming increasingly concerned over their behavior. Was something wrong? Was the ship performing as it should? Or, she thought, was something going on at Pine Creek? She began to have a horrible feeling in her stomach and a sense of foreboding.

As the sun rose at Pine Creek the air was warm, the winds calm, and the coffee cold. Mike was unconscious. You see, when he drifted off to sleep this morning, he began dreaming about whales, particularly humpback whales. He saw the ETs on ribbons of thought enter the whale's mind as he followed them. Except, through his dream, he wasn't entering the whale's mind, but entering his own.

As the ET's ship neared Mike and Kate's home on Pine Creek Road, Kate was extremely concerned. She could feel that something was terribly wrong. They circled around Short Mountain and descended towards Kate and Mike's house. Kate emerged from the ship followed by the guys. Even James T joined them. She ran in the house yelling, "Michael! Michael! Michael!" No answer. Rosie thought, ~He is outside down below.~ She turned and looked at Rosie, then ran down the stairs, through the family room, and out onto the patio. There sat Mike in the chaise lounge surrounded by the ETs. Mike was not moving.

"What's happened? What's going on here?" Kate shouted. Satchmo turned, looked at Kate and thought, ~He is within without assistance.~ In a frantic voice, Kate asked, "Within? Within? What does that mean? What have you done to Mike?"

~He has entered his own mind and is in the place of pure positive emotion. He will not be coming out.~

"Not be coming out?! What do you mean, 'not coming out'?" Kate yelled.

Rosie stepped towards Kate. ~He will eventually cease to exist. He will not sustain his body with nourishment nor hydration.~

This is crazy, Kate thought. Can't these guys do anything about this? They certainly seem to do everything else.

"All right, one of you must go inside Mike and get him out. It's as simple as that," Kate said firmly. The ETs looked at one another and Satchmo thought, ~We cannot enter Mike's mind. In humans, there are too many emotions for us to successfully proceed into Mike's or any other human's mind.~

"You've been tweaking our minds since you guys showed up that morning last spring. What is the difference now?" Kate asked. No answer. This can't be happening Kate thought. Mike is just going to sit there and die of starvation and lack of water? This is unbelievable. When I left this morning, she thought, everything was wonderful; now tragedy. She bent down with her hands over her eyes and began to weep and sob. There was no holding back.

After a moment, Satchmo thought, ~You may enter and try to save Mike. I will help navigate you." Kate took her hands away and looked down at Satchmo. She stopped crying. With no hesitation, Kate asked, "What do I need to do?"

Satchmo led Kate to the outside of Mike's mind with many colorful ribbons leading in. ~Choose this path to follow into his mind. It will lead you on your journey to where Mike is located. He is in the part of the human brain that supports emotions. It is called the limbic system, a set of brain structures beneath the temporal lobe of the cerebrum. You will not need to search for Mike. This area of the mind will draw you in. Beware. You will find it extremely difficult to resist. Success to you.~ And with that, Kate was on her own riding a pathway into Mike's mind.

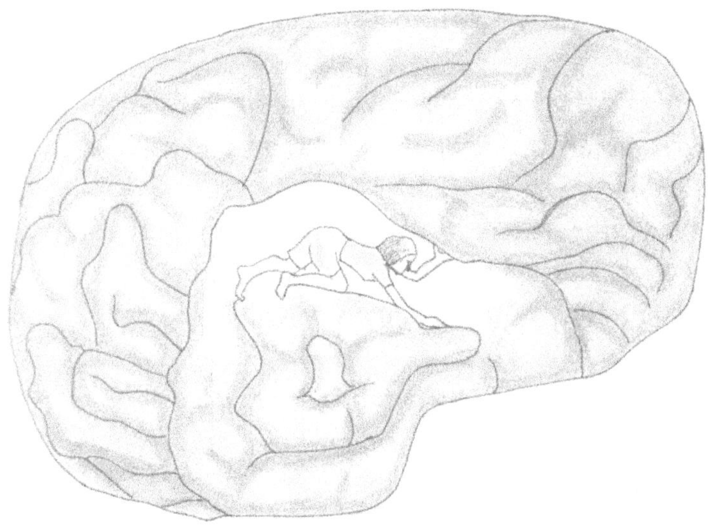

Like giving a horse its head, Kate drifted in Mike's mind, slowly being drawn towards the limbic system. It was eerily haunting. Her surroundings were like a thick fog with a reddish-pink hue. She passed shadows of obscure objects and shapes as she approached Mike. Kate was beginning to feel the allure of being in a place of pure, positive, warming emotion. This is not going to be easy, she thought. Kate began to call out, "Michael, Mike."

Mike was in the lap of luxury feeling absolutely wonderful. He didn't understand why the ETs took him back to the humpback whale's mind, but he didn't care. They're just wonderful guys for arranging this for him. Maybe it's payback for what he's done for them so far.

"Michael." What was that, Mike thought? That sounded like Kate. What would she be doing here? Did the guys arrange that, too? "Kate, is that you? Did you come to join me? Isn't it just a great feeling being here?" Mike happily asked.

Relieved that she had found Mike, she slowly approached, but tried to keep a healthy distance away. Okay, she had found Mike, now what? "Mike, are you all right?"

"Absolutely couldn't be better. Come on in and enjoy the wonderful feelings."

Kate said, "Mike, you shouldn't have entered your own mind. You've put your life in danger. I've come to take you back and get you to the outside."

"What are you talking about? I never entered my own mind. The ETs brought me here again." Mike explained.

"Again? They've taken you inside your mind before?" asked Kate, incredulously.

"No, not my mind, the humpback whale's mind."

Kate thought, none of this makes any sense. Why is Mike insisting he's in a whale's mind?

"Mike, let's back up. What do you remember before the ETs brought you here? Remember, I've been with them today for the past nine hours."

"Well, after you left I decided to pour myself a cup of coffee and watch the sunrise. It was such a beautiful morning. I sat down in the chaise lounge, closed my eyes and began thinking how the ETs seem to know things about me, you, and our boys. It seems I started to doze off when they came and took me to the humpback whale. And here I am. How did you get here?"

"Mike, I am not in the mind of a whale. I am in your mind and if I can't get you out you are going to die a terrible death."

As if waking up from his dream, which he was, the gravity of the situation was starting to become apparent to Mike. He had dreamt of going into the whale's mind, but was in his own mind instead? Was what Kate said true? If the ETs had been with her the last nine hours, then they did not take him into the mind of a whale. This horrible realization was slowly making more sense to Mike. This was not good, Mike thought. There was no way, he knew, that he was coming out.

While Kate was waiting for Mike to sort things out she could feel herself slipping towards Mike in the limbic system and certain doom. It was becoming harder and harder to resist.

"Kate, get yourself out of here and save yourself!" Mike pleaded. "I just can't move from this spot. The emotional attraction is way too strong. Please, save yourself! Turn around and get out while you still can!"

"I am not leaving here without you. I love you, you love me. Think of our boys. Think of your grandchildren. You do want to see them again, don't you? You need to extend your mind towards mine so I can begin taking us out of here." Kate knew the time for action was now. Otherwise, they would certainly both be lost.

All of this personal emotional weight fell on Mike with a powerful, positive effect. Like in the Crystals, when he didn't think he would get out, he found a new resolve. He would try to duplicate that resolve here. He tried reaching towards Kate as she reached for him. She made the proper connection with Mike and began pulling back out of the limbic system. This is extremely difficult, thought Kate. It was like dragging someone up a hill. The emotional drain of the limbic system was taking its toll on Kate. She felt some progress, but began losing the battle.

"Michael, help me, help us! I cannot do this by myself. Push! Come towards me. I'm losing my grip on you and being pulled into the limbic system, too."

"I'm sorry, but I can't anymore," said Mike. He sounded very tired. "I can't. Let go and save yourself."

"Michael, I'm going to give one last pull to get us out of here. But, I need your help. Please! Feel my grip on you. Begin to pull yourself towards me. Here we go. Now, push!"

With all her might, Kate pulled Mike and tried to push against the limbic system. She could feel they were making some progress. "Come on Mike!" she yelled. "I can feel we're moving a little. Push! Push!"

And then suddenly, it was over. Exhausted, Kate lost her connection with Mike and lost her grip on herself. She was being pulled in. The reality of their situation took hold. She had failed.

Oh no, it's over, she thought. I tried. The lure of the limbic system was just too strong. No wonder Mike couldn't help. She soon felt Mike's presence and began connecting with him emotionally. At least we will be together in our final moments, she thought.

As she connected with Mike, she felt something attach to her. ~Do not let go of each other!~ Satchmo thought, and pulled Kate and Mike out of the limbic system and out of Mike's mind.

Satchmo was standing next to Kate, who was standing next to me in the lounge chair. Satchmo opened its eyes first, or whatever they do in absence of eye lids. Kate slowly opened her eyes and looked around. We're back at Pine Creek, she thought! She was relieved, tired, and grateful. She saw Satchmo and turned to it. She tried picking Satchmo up to give him a huge hug, but the ETs were very dense and surprisingly heavy. Instead she bent down and gave Satchmo a big hug.

Standing up and looking at Satchmo, Kate said, "You said you couldn't come inside a human's mind." Satchmo looked up at Kate and gave a little shrug of the shoulders. She bent over again, hugged Satchmo and said, "Thank you so much!" and kissed Satchmo's slit.

Kate stood up, turned around and saw that my eyes weren't open. With some concern, she asked, "Rosie, how come Mike's eyes are still shut?"

"I'm exhausted," I said. "Come and give me a big hug and a kiss before I get jealous of Satchmo." Kate promptly kissed me and gave me a bear hug. She wasn't letting go.

Kate whispered in my ear, "How did you know I kissed Satchmo? Your eyes were closed."

"I was squinting keeping an eye on you and the ETs ," I revealed.

Then Rosie asked, ~What is a dream?~

5

"Time's Fun When You're Having Flies"

-anonymous reptile

Coffee time, a sacred morning tradition beginning around 6:30 in the morning. Kate and I will sit in bed drinking our two cups of coffee to begin the day. The guidelines of coffee time are: try to talk about positive things, keep the subjects upbeat, and try not to talk about the in-laws. If the conversation strays a touch, one of us will remind the other that it is coffee time, get back on a positive track.

This morning Kate was getting herself ready to substitute teach at the local elementary school's kindergarten class. So I am by myself. But instead of bed, I'm sitting in the antique oak rocking chair in the living room looking at the view. I'm wearing my bathrobe while drinking coffee. We have two picture windows that overlook a beautiful small mountain valley. There is a seasonal creek that runs through the field below with towering hills on all sides. Our land runs up to and along Pine Creek Road, a county road that divides the valley. The other side of the road is owned by our neighbor. Their home is an older two-story farm house with the old-style huge red barn that's next to the house. With over 500 acres of grassland, they lease their land to a cattle rancher from Brewster. The rancher brings in herds of cattle to graze all summer and fall.

About a year ago, I was sitting in the same spot having my morning coffee watching a thunder storm that was about twenty miles away. The lightning was spectacular and the thunder deafening. Once again, Kate was getting ready to substitute teach. She walked by me and said, "You know, during a thunder storm you should be seated at least fifteen feet away from any window." I responded smugly by saying, "Then maybe you ought to back up from the living room windows." It wasn't thirty seconds later that a bolt of lightning flashed just in front of our home and crossed in front of the neighbor's barn. The lightning bolt struck just by their house and immediately started a grass fire. I yelled at Kate, "There's a fire at Anderson's. Call 9-1-1!"

With the help of a fire engine and crew, the blaze was out within a half an hour. Now, I'm a believer.

"DING DONG!"

Ding Dong?! Who on earth would be ringing our doorbell at 7:00 a.m.? I got up, put my coffee cup on the kitchen counter and walked to the front door. I looked out the front door window, but didn't see anyone. I opened the door. Looking down, there was Rosie standing on our front porch. Rosie, yep, who on earth indeed. A sickening feeling went to the pit of my stomach.

~Salutations,~ thought Rosie.

~Good morning,~ I thought. ~Would you like to come in?~ What's the deal with this? Usually they're showing up next to your bed at night or hopping out of showers scaring the crap out of everybody. "Oh Kate," I shouted towards our bedroom, "We have an out-of-this-world visitor."

I walked into the living room as Rosie followed. ~Rosie, have a seat in the leather chair there while I pour myself a little more coffee.~ Rosie sat properly in the chair with its' butt forward, both feet on the floor, and arms and hands resting on the tops of his legs.

~So what do we owe the honor of your presence here this morning?~ I thought.

~Do you want to know why I am here?~ Rosie asked.

~Yes Rosie,~ I thought, ~Why are you here?~

~You were 94.7% accurate in the assessment of our craft. It is bio-gravitational-[illegible]-engineered. It is sentient. It approves of you.~

~So, it is biological. Anything else about it?~ I asked.

~Humans have spent a long time studying and utilizing the electro-magnetic spectrum and three dimensional figures. There are other spectrums just as there are other dimensions. Hence, our craft,~ Rosie explained.

~You mean like a space-time continuum thing?~ I thought.

~We do not think of time like humans do. We do not belong to a society that uses time as a means of population control.~

Well, this conversation was beyond me. But it could explain why the Laws of Motion seemingly do not exist once you were inside their ship. ~So let me get this straight. You guys experience other spectrums and dimensions, but can't figure out how to reproduce?~ I asked.

Rosie hesitated a moment. ~Once again, we believe that answer lies in the Crystal Creation which we cannot visit. But now, you can.~ There goes my stomach again. Suddenly, the coffee didn't taste very good. I put my cup down on the coffee table and stared at Rosie. Finally, I asked, ~Are you suggesting I go back in the Crystals to find out how you ETs reproduce?~

~Yes,~ Rosie responded. My deal with the devil called Rosie. That win-win agreement with them while visiting the whale didn't seem so great anymore. I think I'm being hustled-- by a professional.

~Do you realize there is something in the Crystals that's vile, putrid, evil, and seems determined to bring my life to a swift end?!~ I exclaimed.

Rosie adjusted its body in the leather chair until it faced squarely with mine. ~You were in the Crystal Creation for more time than was required to fulfill the answer to your historical question. The time to acquire the knowledge of our reproduction will be minimal. It is a matter of engaging any one of the crystal plates. The information we seek will be placed automatically and immediately in your mind. Then you will return to us where we will retrieve that information from you.~

~How are you so sure this is how it's going to happen? You've never been inside the Crystals,~ I thought.

~When you returned from the Crystal Creation last time, we felt your mind. All four of us determined that this is how information from the crystals is transmitted. Once again, the time will be minimal,~ Rosie stated.

Just then Kate walked by the living room from the bedroom hallway. She looked very professional for her day of subbing in kindergarten: slip-on leather shoes, black slacks from Macy's, a black and white striped long-sleeved shirt with a high collar. Before retiring, Kate had taught in kindergarten for thirty-four years and loved every minute of it. And, by the way she looked this morning, she was going to love every minute of it today.

On her way by, she looked over at us. A touch startled, she stopped. "Oh, good morning, uh..."

"Rosie," I said.

"Rosie," she finished. "How are you this morning?"

~Acceptable~, Rosie thought.

"Very nice," Kate said. Wow, she must be getting the hang of thought talk.

"Well, I'm off to school," she said, "Any flying saucers blocking the driveway?"

Rosie just sat there as I said, "I think you'll be fine. Have a nice day."

"You, too.... I hope," she answered as she opened the door to the garage and left.

As the door shut, I began to think about what Rosie had thought. It was true I had spent a lot of time orienting myself on how I could access information from the crystal plates. But I was trying to get the information in ways I understood: pictures, sounds, and live-action. Not to mention my episodes with the castle and sailing on a sampan. Really, all I had to do was enter the Crystals, engage a crystal plate, gather the information in my mind, and get out. If what Rosie thought was true, the excursion would be like, five seconds or so. And then hopefully, I would be done.

~How do I access information about you from a crystal plate? Is there like a user-name or a password I can use?~ I asked.

~You will use what we are called. We have told you we are observers. However, in our existence we are referred to as

 ~.

~Then for me, will it all be over? Finished?~ I asked.

The answer was, ~The mission would be completed.~

~When?~

Rosie looked up at me, stood up and began walking to the front door. ~Follow me,~ Rosie commanded. Jeez Rosie, at least be polite about it. At that moment, Rosie stopped, turned around, looked at me and thought, ~Please.~ Now that was a first.

As Rosie approached the front door, it swung open on its' own. We stepped outside and the door closed behind us. How does Rosie do that? Lumpy, Satchmo, and even James T, were standing there on the front lawn petting the dogs. What were they all doing outside their ship, I wondered? As Rosie walked towards our barn, it thought, ~One of the things you were accurate about was that we do require, as you described, recharging. As part of this process, we require to be inactive for a period of time. This will happen very soon. In normal situations this inactivity would take place in our moon sanctuary.~ Lumpy, Satchmo, James T and the dogs followed us.

We came to the end of the hay pile by the lean-to. ~We will be inactive here,~ Rosie thought. Then Rosie looked directly at me. ~We acknowledge there is considerable risk involved for you in helping us with this mission. While we are inactive, our craft is yours to travel anywhere you prefer, but only on this planet.~

"What?!" I exclaimed. "You mean I can go wherever I like on earth in your craft while you're in sleep-mode?"

~During inactivity, yes.~

I thought for a moment. ~How long are you inactive?~ I asked.

~Approximately six of your hours,~ Rosie thought.

After doing a little math in my head, I determined I had plenty of time to go to Bermuda, see my oldest son and grandchildren, have a couple rum swizzles, and return before Kate got home or the guys here woke up. ~Rosie, guys, I am going to take you up on your offer,~ I thought confidently.

No response. ~I thought I'll take you up on your offer,~ I thought again. Still no response. I waved my hand in front of Rosie's eyes; no reaction. They were already in sleep-mode. I looked down at Billy and Sammie and said, "Wow. I've got the keys to the old man's car."

I threw my bathrobe on the living room couch and hurriedly walked to our bedroom. In a cotton cloth bag (no zipper), I packed a t-shirt, shorts, and flip-flops. I left a note for Kate on the kitchen counter. “Hey Kate, I borrowed the guys’ flying saucer and am off to Bermuda to see Trav and the grandkids. I should be back before dinner time. And oh, the guys are in sleep-mode by the barn lean-to. XOX, Mike.” I’ve never written that before. I walked out the front door using the door knob, gave the dogs a pet on the head, and approached the ET’s craft. Reaching up with cloth bag in hand, I entered the ship.

I’ve been in this ship three times, but this time it was different. Of course the guys weren’t here, but I could feel something else, something different—a presence. It had to be the ship itself. I looked around inside. As always, there was no instrumentation, no visible means of controls to operate the ship. How am I supposed to pilot this thing? Then it occurred to me. I might have to get things started by using my mind. I thought, ~Bermuda is our destination.~ Immediately, we climbed and accelerated into the eastern morning sky. A smile began to form on my face. Hey, this is great. I'll surprise my son and grandkids with an impromptu visit and have a rum swizzle or two. Yep, this is going to be great! Mike, I told myself, once again sit back, relax, and enjoy the short, non-stop flight to Bermuda.

As we broke through some scattered clouds, I began thinking about what Rosie had said earlier, that there were other spectrums and dimensions, hence their craft. Was this ship not of this universe? Was it created in an other-worldly place? If it was, that could answer so many questions, like how does this thing travel so fast through our atmosphere or why the Laws of Motion don't apply inside their ship? I wondered if I, a human, could safely visit another dimension. If so, what would it be like, or probably, not like? What an experience that would be. It would be fun to give it a try sometime.

As I'm thinking about the possibilities of other dimensions and spectrums, the surroundings in the ship suddenly began to darken. Eventually, it became totally black. This has never happened before. I looked around for any signs of light; nothing. Has something gone wrong with the ship? Have we entered outer space? I searched for stars, planets, and galaxies outside of the ship. Nothing.

And then, as if a dimmer switch was slowly being turned on, I began to see wisps of what appeared to be smoke, water vapor, or a type of mist. They were all in front of me. The wisps of smoke slowly traveled by me. As I looked at the mist, I began to see images of people; folding, turning, twisting amongst the vapors. And then I realized that a lot of these people I'm witnessing were

Rosie sat properly in the chair with his butt forward, both feet on the floor, and arms and hands resting on the tops of his legs Lumpy, Satchmo, James T, and the dogs followed us. We came to the end of the hay pile by the lean-to. ~We will be inactive here,~ No response. ~I thought I'll take you up on your offer,~ I me and the ETs; one image was of Rosie and me sitting in my living room, then the image folded in on itself and disappeared. The next image was the guys under the lean-to, but it quickly changed to me getting into their ship. I tried to reach out to touch the mist. Like an image in a 3-D movie, there was nothing there. In fact, I tried looking at my arms, legs, and body. There was nothing there, either.

I began wondering why this was all of a sudden happening, pictures of me and the guys on wisps of mist just floating by in what could be described as clouds. Just before these clouds of images began floating by, I was thinking what Rosie had thought, about other dimensions and spectrums. Is this another dimension I'm in right now? But why is this happening? Then I remembered Rosie telling me that the ship is sentient. Did the ship feel my thoughts, read my mind and decided to introduce me to another dimension? You know, nothing happened when I originally boarded the ship until I thought of our destination. Maybe it's the same situation, thinking something and the ship reacting.

~In a dimensional time shift, these are your experiences with the Observers.~

The ship! I'd been thinking about how cool it would be to visit another dimension. Be careful what you wish for, I thought. These guys are way too literal.

~Hello,~ I thought, ~Is this the ship? The bio-gravitational--engineered craft?~

~Yes.~

~I just experienced seeing what happened this morning with Rosie, in what appears to be like a time cloud of swirling mist or fog-like wisps with images of the near past. Can I assume I will be seeing the Observers rescue Kate and me from the inside of my mind soon?~

~Yes.~

~So I'm going to observe every time I've had experiences with the Observers in the past?~ I asked.

~Yes.~

~And can I sit back and relax and enjoy watching all the times I've been with Rosie and the guys?~

~No.~

Uh ho. ~Why not?~ I asked. ~Can't humans survive in a different dimension?~

~You are safe as long as you want to stay,~ was the answer.

~So ship, what am I missing here?~ I asked. ~Am I or am I not safe here?~

~To return to your spacial-time frame of reference, you must meld with your mind in the, as you describe, time clouds. If you do not attach to what's already happened to you, I cannot bring you back to the present in me.~

~Jeez, ship or craft or whatever the Observers call you, all I want to do is go to Bermuda and see my son and grandchildren! Please get me out of this time warp situation I am in!~ I shouted. No answer. I pleaded again with the ship to return me to my present time. Again, no answer.

Well, all right. I've missed one opportunity to connect my mind with my mind in the time clouds, but there should be four more chances coming my way. I have to be patient, alert, and ready. I looked around at my surroundings with my minds-eye. I was in a mist or fog-like space, but there was no sensation of moisture. The color, if you call it that, was a battle-ship grey. There was nothing else here.

As I looked at what seemed to be straight ahead of me, another eerie wisp of vapors or mist was coming my way. Once again, the vapor-like entity was turning, twisting and folding in on itself, making identification of the figures and their surroundings difficult. For a moment, I saw myself sitting on the chase lounge with Rosie, Satchmo, James T,

There sat Mike in the chaise lounge surrounded by the ETs. Mike was not moving.

"What's happened? What's going on here?" Kate shouted. Satchmo turned, looked at Kate and thought, ~He is within without assistance.~ In a frantic voice, Kate asked, "Within? Within? What does that mean? What have you done to Mike?"

and Kate standing around me.

As it approached, I began trying to find mind waves from my image to connect with. I couldn't do it. The time ripples made it difficult to latch on to. It was like on TV when you see a search party out in the woods at night. Everyone has a flashlight. The flashlight's beams seem to go everywhere or deflect off of trees, the ground, or diffused in tree limbs and bushes. Not any pathways of emotion seemed to be pointed straight in my direction. Eventually, the time cloud floated by and out of my reach. This is going to be harder than I thought. Okay, three chances left; be patient, be focused. I can do this, I can get out of here.

The whale and Crystal Creation came and went. One thing I learned was that the stronger my emotion was in the time cloud, the closer I came to latching on. These emotional waves were strongest during heightened emotions from me. When the ETs were in the shower and scared the crap out of me, when I was in the whale's mind enjoying positive emotions, and when I barely got out of the Crystals were all times when the pathways were strongest. But the twisting and turning, and spiraling of the time mist made it extremely difficult to make a mind connection. Either my inexperience with mind melds or lack of mental agility made it seemingly impossible. In other words, I needed practice, lots of practice. But with two more tries, I must learn quickly. I'm like a frustrated surfer trying to catch a good wave. And besides all of that, I am becoming mentally tired and exhausted.

Italy, St. Peter's Lutheran Church, the moon, and the Crystal Creation time cloud had come and gone. When a mind wave appears, it almost immediately disappears. This time though, something was unusual. I began to feel another presence, a stronger one when trying to attach to myself. This presence has to be one of the ETs. Who else could it be? Maybe I can use this on my final attempt to get out of this space-time dimension. But which ET? Immediately, I thought it had to be Rosie. Rosie is always closest to me, does almost all of the communication with me, and seems to be the one that makes a lot of their decisions. If I concentrate on Rosie and connect with it I can then, from Rosie, attach to my own mind in the time cloud. Otherwise,

I don't know what else to do. It was virtually impossible to catch a wave to myself by the way the time cloud goes in and out, folding in on itself and shifting up and down. I am frustrated, tired, and becoming afraid. I do not want to spend the rest of my life in this space-time-dimension. But now I have some hope. I have a plan for my last chance.

It doesn't take too long for the last time cloud to appear. As the mist twists and turns, I can see us out in the front yard and driveway. Then I see the Seahawks stadium. Mars comes into view, then folds away. When the front lawn reappears with all of us standing under their ship, I made a grab with my mind to Rosie's mind. Nothing. There is nothing there. I tried again when I saw us flying to Seattle. Again, I have missed the mark. The time cloud is slowly moving too far away for me to link up. I calculated that I had one more shot. I waited for the moment when we were shaking hands shortly before they boarded their ship. I can sense myself, but the wave was too weak. I do sense Rosie's though, my last chance. With all the mind power I could generate, I made a final stab. I have it! I actually entered Rosie's mind! I had made the connection! Now to attach with myself from Rosie. But, it wasn't happening. For some reason, I couldn't go from Rosie's mind to my own. Why not? This plan was working so well. And then, the horrible realization strikes me! It wasn't Rosie after all! But who was it? I made a fleeting mind glance at the

Even though it was a moon-lit night, I could see out of the ship like it was daytime. We cleared the Cascade Mountains heading to Puget Sound. We flew over Whidbey Island, Edmonds, Bay and suddenly stopped, over the Seattle Seahawks' Lumen Field. ~A familiar landmark for you, ~ thought Rosie. ship began to slow down and finally stopped. Mars was right there in front of us: huge, brilliant, astounding, humbling. was Olympus Mons and the three shield v olcanoes to the west. One of the shield volcanoes was p artially overed in clouds. Looking to the east, like a huge open tear in the middle of the planet, was Valle Marinais, the largest canyon in the solar system. I could As I lowered out of their ship, our dogs, Bill and Sammie, came other ETs. Oh my god, it was Lumpy! Lumpy!? Why Lumpy?! I'm too late. The time cloud had moved beyond my reach.

What a mistake I had made! I thought back and it was always Rosie I communicated with, only occasionally Satchmo. Evidently, that left Lumpy free to enter my mind undetected, for whatever reason. How stupid could I have been! If I had shoulders, they would be drooping right now.

I am worn out and totally exhausted. All I feel is despair—utter and overwhelming despair.

6

A Nightmare on Humphrey Street

For six years my parents would pack up we three boys in the '53 Chevy pickup in October and make the arduous journey from Clinton on Whidbey Island to east of the mountains. Eventually we would arrive in the small country town of Tonasket. From there, it was at least another hour until we arrived at the campsite by Lost Lake. It was just over a 250 mile trek. I remembered mom would wake us up in the dark and we would arrive at Lost Lake in the dark. In those days Stevens Pass was a series of switch backs and narrow roads. Many roads in Eastern Washington were still gravel. Since there wasn't a lot of room in the cab of the pickup, my oldest brother would ride in the back under a crude, canvas canopy. The dust was so bad on one of the primitive roads that he had to jump off the truck to avoid choking to death. All of this so dad could go deer hunting.

But hunting season in 1959 was going to be different. My brothers were staying with friends in Clinton and I was staying at my Aunt Molly's. I had several wonderful aunts, but Molly was special. We had so much fun together. And she would do almost anything. Molly was my favorite aunt. I adored her.

Hunting season seemed to always fall on Halloween. This year was no different. But instead of going Trick or Treating, I was going to help Molly pass out candy at her home. She lived on Humphrey Street, a busy road in Clinton. Every year she would get twenty to thirty Trick-or-Treaters on Halloween. This year they started knocking on Molly's door about 5:00 p.m. We were busy handing out boxes of Cracker Jacks until about 8:30 that night when the stream of Trick-or-Treaters came to an end.

I walked into the living room from the foyer that was by the front door. Molly's husband, Oliver, was sitting in his chair smoking cigarettes and watching TV. The living room was filled with a smoky haze. It was a school night. I was tired and said goodnight to Olly. I went to the bathroom and then walked into the guest bedroom. Molly tucked me in bed and said to have sweet dreams. I looked at the Baby Ben clock on the night stand. It was 9:10 p.m. Molly had left the hall light on and cracked the door open just enough to let in some light. As my eyes adjusted to the darkness, I looked around the bedroom. The walls and ceiling were beige in color. Hanging on one of the walls was the inevitable picture of flowers in a vase on a table. To the right of the foot of the bed was a chest of drawers standing about five feet tall. There was a shaded window in the wall on the right of the bed. And to the right of my head was a wooden, stand-up wardrobe closet with two narrow doors. I shut my eyes. All was good. I immediately fell asleep to the tick-tock of the wind-up clock.

Sometime during the night in my dream-sleep, I could hear voices. I couldn't make out what was being said, but I could definitely hear a conversation going on. As I slowly woke up from a sound sleep, the first thing I saw was the Baby Ben clock on the night stand. It looked like the time was 2:46 a.m. What would Molly and Olly be doing up now talking in the living room?

As my eyes adjusted to the bedroom light, I looked around. I realized the voices weren't coming from the living room. The voices were in my bedroom! I looked for the source and saw two figures sitting on top of the chest of drawers. They didn't have legs or feet. But from the waist up, they were on top of the chest of drawers. Surrounding them was a kind of smoke or haze. Had Olly been in here smoking? Because of the haze, their facial features weren't very discernable. And then I suddenly realized they were talking to me!

"And you know, Mike, if you were to come with us there are all kinds of things to play with, all sorts of toys."

The other figure said, "Yes, and we know you like science. It's your favorite subject at school. If you come with us, there are endless fun science experiments you can do. We also know you're really into aviation and airplanes and helicopters. Space travel really fascinates you, too. We can't tell you how many airplanes, helicopters, model rockets and space ships there are where we live that you can play with. You would have so much fun if you would just come with us."

That was it. I jumped out of bed, busted out the bedroom door and ran into the living room yelling, “Molly, Molly, Molly!”

Molly and Olly quickly came out of their bedroom and found me on the living room couch dressed in my striped pajamas and white socks. They wanted to know what was going on. I was so excited and frightened, it was hard to explain what had taken place. I told them there were two men in my bedroom wanting me to go with them.

Where do they want to take you, they asked?

I said I don’t know.

Well, first Molly and Olly tried to comfort me. Molly sat next to me on the couch rubbing my leg. Molly explained that I was in an unfamiliar home with odd creaking’s and house noises that I wasn’t used to. And after all, it was Halloween. I was just having a bad dream and everything was all right. Olly went and inspected the guest bedroom and said everything was just fine, no one was there. So after some more soothing talk and several hugs, I went back in the guest bedroom. Molly tucked me in again and I put my head under the covers and closed my eyes. It was just a bad dream, I told myself, just a bad dream.

Talking. Oh, no! I opened my eyes and slowly pulled down the covers from my head. There they were on the chest of drawers again. Each one continued to let me know that if I followed them I would have so much fun. I felt the urge to shout at Molly to come in here, but I didn’t really want to bother her and Olly again. Jeez, what was I going to do?

Just then, the doors to the standing wardrobe closet opened. I looked over and saw a man step out. He was dressed in black pants and black shoes. He had on a white shirt with a black bow-tie. His dress coat had vertical red and white stripes. On his head was a flat-brimmed straw hat and in his right hand was a black cane.

“Young man,” he says to me as he slaps the cane on the palm of his left hand, “I have just come from a grand carnival with hundreds of exciting rides, clowns of all kinds, exotic animals, foods of all sort, and some of your favorite candies.” He took his cane and pointed towards the closet door. “This grand carnival is something you can attend right now! All you have to do is follow me into the closet."

For the second time that night, I ran into the living room shouting Molly's name. And for the rest of the night, I slept with Molly and Olly slept in the guest bedroom.

7

Time for this One to Come Home

I need sleep. I'm exhausted. I wonder if I can close my mind's eye. After a couple tries, unfortunately, it wasn't happening. I still saw the battle-ship grey mist all around me.

All right. Before I panic and stick needles in my mind's eye, I need to take stock of the situation. The ship has told me I must meld with my mind in one of the time clouds before it can bring me back. I've seen five time clouds. I've tried to attach myself with myself each time. Because of the undulation of each time cloud, I have been unable to grasp my wave length in the cloud. My last chance was hooking up with Rosie when we all first met. I did hook up with Rosie to find out it was Lumpy instead. And as I saw it, there were no more options. Where's that needle?

As the grim truth presented itself, there appeared to be a blurry object slowly approaching me. Was my mind's eye so tired that I'm really not seeing anything at all? I kept looking in the thick, grey mist. There was definitely something headed my way.

Soon, it was recognizable as a time cloud like the ones I had witnessed earlier. The images inside the cloud were twisting, turning, and folding in upon itself. It was extremely hard to make out anything about the images. And then I saw a child in bed. Soon he gets out of the bed and runs. Before the image twists away, I saw an older woman on a couch next to the boy. Oh my god! It was my Aunt Molly and me! It doesn't take me long to realize the horrible implications. It was the ETs in the

That was it. I jumped out of bed, busted out the bedroom door and ran into the living room yelling, "Molly, Molly, Molly!" Molly sat next to me on the couch rubbing my leg. Molly explained that I was in an unfamiliar home with odd creaking's and house noises that I wasn't used to. And after all, it was Halloween. I was just having a bad dream and everything was all right. Olly went and inspecte d the guest bedroom and said everyt hing.

guest bedroom
were trying to take
almighty, they
with me fifty years
always known it
nightmare that
knew for sure.
thinking about this
experience, I
that I've got
another chance to
spatial-time
don't run out of
but twice. And that
fifty years ago, my
running extremely

Okay, I told
ready and look into
the cloud for any
younger self
bedroom a second
there was nothing
the cloud. The
blurred and
There was the red
coat. No, now it
looking, but it
taking too long.
to miss my second

And then
wisp of time mist, I
myself running
living room yelling,
mind, I reached
old mind's

Talking. Oh, no! I opened my eyes and slowly pulled down the covers from my head. There they were on the chest of drawers again. Each one continued to let me know that if I followed them I would have so much fun. I felt the urge to shout at Molly to come in here, but I didn't really want to bother her and Olly again. Jeez, what was I going to do?

Just then, the doors to the standing wardrobe closet opened. I looked over and saw a man step out. He was dressed in black pants and black shoes. He had on a white shirt with a black bow-tie. His dress coat had vertical red and white stripes. On his head was a flat-brimmed straw hat and in his right hand was a black cane.

"Young man," he says to me as he slaps the cane on the palm of his left hand, "I have just come from a grand carnival with hundreds of exciting rides, clowns of all kinds, exotic animals, foods of all sort, and some of your favorite candies." He took his cane and pointed towards the closet door.

"This grand carnival is something you can attend right now! All you have to do is follow me into the closet."

For the second time that night, I ran into the living room shouting Molly's name.

that night. They
me away. God
were messing
ago! I've
wasn't a
night. Now I

As I kept
terrible
suddenly realized
another chance,
get out of this
dimension. I
the bedroom once,
evening
emotions were
high.

myself, get
the mist of
images of my
running out of the
time. As I looked,
recognizable in
images were
twisting. Wait.
and white striped
was gone. I kept
seemed to be

Am I going
and final chance?
on the trailing
momentarily see
again into the
"Molly!" With my
out to my 9-year-
pathway. I

missed it. Damn it. Like an angle worm on a fish hook, the wave keeps squirming around. Wait, my younger self yells "Molly" again. I reached out fast and sure. Got it! I finally got hold of my nine-year-old mind.

I stayed motionless for a moment. The relief of what had just happened washed over me. Finally, I thought, ~Mr. Wizard. I don't want to be in a time-warp dimension any more. Bring me home Mr. Wizard, bring me home.~

The ship, Mr. Wizard, dropped me off at a small park in Northeast Bermuda close to my son's home. As we descended out of the sky, I saw that the park was deserted. As my feet touched the grass, my body crumpled to the ground, and I immediately fell asleep.

Something poked my right shoulder. What was that? In a moment, I felt another. My eyes slowly opened. First I saw green grass, then a structure next to me, a Jungle Gym. Where was I, I wondered? Another poke. I turned my head to the right. I saw the shaded silhouettes of three young boys with the sun directly behind them. One had a soccer ball between his right forearm and side.

"You okay mister?" one of them asked.

"Where am I?"

"This is a park by Ducks Puddle Drive and Coney Island Road," was the response.

"Yeah, but where am I?"

"You're in St. George's parish in Bermuda."

Now memories started to flood back. I looked around and sat up. I realized I had no clothes on. I saw my cotton bag beside the Jungle Gym and reached for it. "Men, I want to thank you for checking on me. I've been on a long journey and needed to rest for a while. I appreciate you waking me up. Now, if you will turn around, I need to get dressed and finish my travels."

"You're welcome," they said, turned around and began walking off through the park.

Jeez, how long had I been asleep? Was it too late to see Trav and the grandkids? I stood up, dressed, and began heading across the park to Coney Island Road. Fortunately, the three boys were the only ones in the park. I walked up to the road. There were no houses around, a very rural part of Bermuda. If I took a right I'd end up at the cricket fields, grandstands, and an older home converted into a restaurant called The Jamaican Grill. To the left across the road was the Bermuda Railway Trail, and about a half mile away across North Shore Road was Callen Glen Rise where Trav's home was. I crossed Coney Island Road and began walking down the Bermuda Railway Trail.

Kate and I had been to Bermuda several times visiting Trav and his family and we had walked many miles on the Railway Trail. As you strolled the Trail, here and there you encountered signposts that tell the railroad's history and interesting stories. In 1908, Bermuda outlawed the gasoline engine. But with Bermuda's tourism on the rise and trying to get onions and other produce to market, the idea of a train from one tip of the Bermuda islands to the other was the answer. There were many concrete trestles built in the seawater, several bridges constructed, and many deep cuts had to be made through limestone rock. At only twenty-one miles long, it was probably the most expensive railroad ever built. In October of 1931, "Old Rattle and Shake" began service. Ironically, the train engine used gasoline. It ran for seventeen years. However, because of so many trestles and bridges, the infrastructure maintenance became too expensive and the railroad closed in 1948.

One interesting story about the railroad involved a runaway train. In 1933, the train's engineer feared that the conductor was not on the train. He stuck his head outside of the cab on one side, then the other looking for him. In doing so, he was struck on the head by an obstruction and fell off the train. Picking himself up, he made a phone call from a local home to Dispatch saying there was a runaway train heading for St. George's.

J. Richardson, another engineer who lived in St. George's, was contacted. He was dispatched by cycle to Mullet Bay, where the railroad had an incline. The runaway train slowed down enough for Richardson to hop aboard. After about six minutes of his self-made heroics to slow the train, it arrived in St. George's and came to a stop. Many felt Richardson was just having fun about the whole adventure. Anyway, in 1987, the Bermuda government opened up eighteen miles of the railway trail to walkers and cyclists.

I walked out of the limestone cut and crossed North Shore Road and walked down Callen Glen Rise, about a hundred yards from Trav's home. As I strolled down the road I was surrounded by thick, tall deciduous trees. Most trees had vines growing on them with some wild philodendrons producing huge leaves that leaned out to catch some filtered sun. On the other side of the road was a small ravine. It had a couple palm trees, but hidden below them were about 6 or 7 banana trees, some with bunches of green bananas. A make-shift barbed-wire fence was tacked to trees that surrounded the banana trees to keep unwanted visitors out. Walking to the front door, I gave a couple knocks. It doesn't take long for Trav to answer. He looked at me with a mystified expression and then looked behind me.

"No, no one else, just me. Got a rum swizzle for the old man?" After a handshake and greetings, I asked where the grandchildren were. He explained that I had just missed them. They were spending the evening with friends on the other side of St. David's. I looked at the wall clock in the kitchen. It was 6:25 pm. I had only about thirty minutes left before I was due back to rendezvous with Mr. Wizard. The grandkids were too far away. Oh, well. Trav was still confused about how I showed up on his doorstep out of nowhere. I said I would explain that when I left and "where is that rum swizzle?" I ended up with a Dark and Stormy, just as good.

After catching up on all of the news of each family, it was time to leave. "Okay, come with me to the park by Ducks Puddle Road and I'll show you how I got here," I said. As we walked up to the Jungle Gym in the park, I could see Mr. Wizard hovering and slowly descending. I told Trav to stay by the Jungle Gym as I walked out to an open spot in the park. I turned my back to Trav and began to undress.

"Hey Trav, keep these clothes for me for the next time I come to visit. Take care," I said, and raised my hands up into the ship. As we ascended into the beautiful blue Bermudian sky, I could see Trav saying, "What the f...?"

Mr. Wizard and I arrived back at Pine Creek before Kate got home from school. As we came down to the front lawn, I noticed James T, Lumpy, and Satchmo on the back of Babe. James T had the reigns. Somehow it didn't seem odd or surprising. I gave Mr. Wizard a thank you and fond farewell. But instead of engaging the ETs, I decided to go into the house and have a cocktail.

I came in through the front door, went to the kitchen and crumpled up the note I had left for Kate; no sense causing alarms with her. As I walked by the living room, I saw my bathrobe still on the couch. I put it on, mixed a rum and coke and sat in the oak rocker in the living room. Just then Kate came through the kitchen door from the garage. She took a look at me and said, “Well, I see you’ve accomplished something today. You’ve gone from caffeine to alcohol.”

Jeez, I thought.

“I heard that,” she said.

8

Disasters, Naturally

I felt a nudge in my ribs, then another. “Mike, wake up.” I slowly opened my eyes to see the green, pulsing light coming through the master bathroom window and door. I sighed. “Full circle,” I said. “What time is it?”

“3:33 a.m.,” Kate answered. Ohhhhh. I didn’t like that.

“Look,” Kate said, “Get this done and over with. It’s time for us to move on from the ETs inability to reproduce.” She leaned over and kissed me. “Be safe, I love you, and hurry back.”

I got out of bed. “Do my best and I love you. If Rosie is right, and I think Rosie is, this shouldn’t take very long. Hopefully, I’ll see you soon.” And with that, I left the bedroom, walked down the hallway and went out the front door to a crisp, cool morning. As expected, Lumpy and Satchmo were petting the dogs and Rosie stood looking at me as I approached them.

I walked up and stood in front of Rosie. I looked down into its eyes. ~It was you guys in the bedroom that night over sixty years ago. What was that all about?~ I demanded.

Rosie stared at me for a while and finally thought, ~We were too early. You were not ready.~ I waited for a moment. No apology seemed forthcoming. ~All right, let’s go,~ I thought.

Standing next to one of the giant green crystals, its’ surface never failed to astonish me. It was like pale green metallic paint, except the green metal pieces were moving under the surface. With some reluctance, I touched the crystal’s surface. I found the grey pathway and was quickly inside. I walked down the corridor a ways to give myself a little room on each side of me. I looked into a hexagonal crystal plate directly below my eyes and began mentally visualizing the ET symbols.

Out of nowhere, someone or something picked me up and threw me down the corridor. I landed on my left side about ten feet from where I had been standing. Shaken and surprised, I looked up to see what or who had just done that. All I saw was a wall of pure black swiftly moving towards me. I suddenly felt like I was going to throw up and experienced a terrible feeling of foreboding. I quickly reached up and touched the first plate I could feel. Immediately, I found myself lying in a desert.

I looked around at the landscape. There were some jagged, rocky hills close by with a somewhat circular mound off in the distant horizon. The sky was a brilliant blue with a couple of white cloud wisps. I was surrounded by Joshua trees, Mojave yuccas, and burro brush. Either I was in Joshua Tree National Park or close by. But it was definitely the Mojave Desert. Kate and I had visited there a few years ago. We were somewhat familiar with some of the desert vegetation. I stood up, brushed the sand off my side and legs. The sandy gravel was hot under my feet. I thought to myself, I needed some clothes. I had an idea where I could get some, but I would have to return to the crystals. I did not want to go back to the same corridor I had just left. So what was I going to do? I thought back to the last two times I had entered the surrounding mist. Both times I was in an extreme hurry. I wondered if entering the mist slowly would present more waves to enter the crystals. I wanted to avoid going to where I had just been.

As I was thinking about these possibilities, I began to feel nauseous again with this feeling of doom. The sky started to become dark, almost dusk-like. I looked at the position of the sun and it was almost overhead. Whatever was in the Crystals appeared to have followed me here. I decided not to stick around and find out why. I began to walk slowly into the mist. Yes, there were other pathways that opened up. Randomly, I took one of the waves off to the side and found myself in a totally different corridor in the Crystals with no black.

I looked into one of the crystal plates. I made a connection to where and when I wanted to go to get some clothes. South of the town of Tonasket in Washington was a small community known as Ponderosa Pine Estates. Back in 1984, Kate and I had built a log home there. It was my intention to go to our log home, get inside, and borrow some of my own clothes.

In the crystal plate, the log home came into view. Next to the house should have been a garage. It wasn't there. I had built the garage after our log home was completed. I moved the view a little ahead of time. Yes, there was the garage now and our family dog, Nickie, was in her kennel next to the building. Since she was inside the kennel, that meant everyone else was at school; perfect! I made the connection and was instantly standing in front of the back porch of our log home.

I looked under the porch step. The back door key was hanging on a nail hidden from view. I got the key, stepped up on the porch and walked toward the back door. I slid the key into the door knob, twisted it and entered my old home. I left the key in the door knob. I didn't want to misplace it somewhere in the house. I walked past the laundry room and entered the kitchen. What a weird experience! I walked through the kitchen, past the dining room and went up the staircase to the second floor. At the top of the stairs, I took a right into the master bedroom.

I went over to the oak dresser and pulled open the top drawer. I got out underwear and socks. I opened the closet doors and on the top shelf was a pair of Levis workpants. I grabbed a t-shirt advertising Sun Mountain resort and on the floor of the closet, I found my old favorite pair of Adidas tennis shoes. You know, the kind that are completely broken in and feels so good on your feet. And they still felt great putting them on. Completely clothed, I went downstairs. I paused and took a quick look around the living room. What memories there were here as our boys grew up. Okay, got to go.

I opened the back door and stepped outside. Directly in front of me was me, Kate, Joel, and Nickie; evidently a slight miscalculation concerning the time of day. Where's Trav, I wondered? Oh, there he was coming out of the garage with a couple of books in his hands.

Nickie came forward and looked up at me with those soft, brown eyes. I put the back of my hand out for her to sniff. Instead, she put her head under my hand to be petted. I stroked her head three times and with misty eyes, I looked up and said to everyone, "This will all make sense in about thirty-five years." I turned, stepped off the porch and walked into the mist. As I did, I heard a solitary bark.

Back in the Crystals, I randomly picked one of the plates. I looked down and there was no doubt at what event I was witnessing; The Great Alaskan Earthquake of 1964. I was viewing the famous scene showing parts of the main street in Anchorage that had fallen fifteen feet with cars up-ended and strewn everywhere. The magnitude of the quake was 9.2, making it the strongest earthquake ever in North America and the second strongest world-wide. All right, back to business. Once again I began visualizing and concentrating on the symbols that meant "observers" in the ET's language. After a moment I thought, that's odd, nothing is happening. I kept trying to send the images into the crystal plate expecting to gain access to information about ET reproduction. I still wasn't receiving anything. Do I need to touch this particular plate to find the information I'm looking for? This is taking way too long and besides, I've got some dark entity that's after me trying to do me harm.

In a moment of desperation I lightly touched the crystal as I concentrated on the ET symbols. Immediately, I am knocked down to the ground. To my horror I have been transported to the Anchorage earthquake. The ground is literally rolling like waves on the ocean. The ground waves had to be at least four feet high. Trees looked like windshield wipers, hitting the ground on one side, then turning over and hitting the ground on the other side. As I looked around at my surroundings, it appeared I was at the edge of a city park and next to a residential area that sat on a hillside. In one place I could see the land had formed a huge crack and dropped about eight feet splitting a home in two parts. The whole scene was so surreal. And it was odd, but there seemed to be a ringing sound.

The ground was shaking and rolling so violently that I couldn't stand up. I began crawling to the middle of the park to avoid falling trees. Just then, the ground in front of me split and rose upward about five feet. Under the ground's surface I saw a ruptured pipe and began to smell gas. I hurriedly started climbing up this newly formed bank. I was not getting any traction with my feet. The soil was too sandy. I got as far as I could go, and in desperation, reached up and grabbed some tall grass. Pulling myself up, I was finally on top of the bank. I crawled away from the gas main just as a power pole snapped off at its base sending power lines sparking to the ground. WHOOSH! The gas had ignited sending huge flames skyward. Luckily, the bank I was on was high enough for me to avoid the fire. I heard a crack-snap behind me. I looked back to see the top of a spruce tree breaking off and falling to the ground in front of me, blocking my path to the center of the park. As the top of the tree rolled violently to its side, one of the limbs hit the back of my head sending my face into the grass and darkness.

I woke up on a beach. Dazed, I looked around. It appeared to be low tide, thank god. I sat up. The beach was not shaking or rolling. What happened to the earthquake? The last thing I remembered was getting hit on the back of my head by a tree limb. I rubbed the spot where the limb had struck, but there were no lumps or pain. What's the deal with that? I looked around. The tide was way out. I noticed that there weren't any people anywhere on the beach. No one was beachcombing, playing with dogs, or digging clams. I turned around to look in back of me. Quite a ways from where I was sitting was a small town with a long sea wall in front of it. In the distance were several tree-covered hills and small mountains beyond. There were writings of some kind on a couple of the town buildings. If I had to guess, it looked like Japanese letters or symbols. I was not in Alaska anymore. The temperature was definitely warmer.

Still a little groggy, I finally realized there was a siren going off and on and blinking red lights all along the seawall. What was going on here? I looked back at the beach's horizon. It seemed there was a white line on the horizon. Did I hear a dull roar from there? Extreme low tide, a white line on the sea's horizon that appeared to be growing taller and louder, a siren with blinking red lights along the sea wall on a beach by a coastal Japanese town—oh my god, tsunami!

I got up quickly and began running for the sea wall and high ground. As I ran I had this bad feeling in the pit of my stomach thinking I may not make it in time. The roar was getting louder behind me. Was I going to get to the sea wall before being crushed by the huge wave? I looked behind me. I could see it was getting taller and closer.

Running to the wall, my sixty-year-old legs began to ache. I was gasping trying to catch my breath. Sweat from my forehead was running into my eyes and stinging them. I couldn't see very well. Just then, I ran into a small tidal pool, lost my balance and fell forward. Picking myself up, I looked backwards. Jeez, it was going to be close. As I came up to the sea wall, I couldn't see any steps that would take me to the top. The sea wall seemed to be a mile long, but where were the steps? There's got to be a way to the top of the wall.

I began to hear yelling and screaming. I looked up at the top of the sea wall and saw several people waving their arms and motioning to me to come in their direction. I looked where they were pointing. Sure enough, I could now see a stairway that paralleled the wall. That's why I couldn't see it to begin with. A few seconds later, I turned the corner of the stairs and dashed up to the top.

I was greeted by several people with smiles, greetings, and bows. I smiled and bowed, too, exclaiming many "thank yous". I stood with these people as we watched the huge wave hit the wall. A jolt was felt as the sea water shot straight up in the sky, then fell drenching us all. As the water in the bay calmed somewhat, everyone was thankful that the sea wall had held. There was lots of laughing, smiles, more bows, and happy spirits; all except one older man dressed in black. He was looking out at the sea with a stern look on his face. Finally, he said something in Japanese and pointed out to the sea.

We all looked out to where the old man was pointing. Oh my god, another wave! Except this one was at least five times higher than the first one. I've got to get to higher ground and fast, I thought. I turned and looked behind the town at the hills. That was where I needed to go.

I started running through streets and alleys keeping the hills in the distance as a target when I could see them. There were lots of cars and trucks on the streets which impeded my progress. I dipped into as many alleys as I could to avoid traffic.

I came upon what looked like the town square. If this was a half-way point maybe I can still stay ahead of the second wave and make it to the hills outside of town. Trying not to get hit by traffic, I began crossing the town square. I started hearing splashes with each step I took. I looked down and sea water was flowing in. The color of the water was almost black. At first I thought well, that wasn't so bad. Half way across the square, the sea water was up to my knees. I was hardly moving trying to get to the other side. Suddenly, I was swept off my feet and headed down one of the main streets. Caught in the water current, cars were floating alongside of me. Some still had people in them. Their expressions were of puzzlement and terror. Debris, garbage, and anything that floated was all around. Then it occurred to me; the surging sea is taking me to the other end of town. If I can just keep treading water, I may eventually come to the foothills and high ground. It could be a matter of swimming to a side hill and crawling on it to get above the level of the sea. So instead of fighting the sea water, I thought, just relax and keep my head above water. As I was thinking of my new plan, a body dressed in black drifted by me.

The street narrowed and the sea water became a torrent of racing, churning, black water. I could no longer keep my head above it. The street turned to the right and I was slammed into the wall of a store front. Gasping for air I tried to swim to the surface. Just then the river of water converged with another street. The sea water from this street was bringing with it wood pallets, hundreds of wood pallets. There must be a large loading dock nearby. My head knocked into one, slightly dazing me. I grabbed onto it. Maybe I can pull myself up and use it as a type of raft. I soon became surrounded by pallets making it impossible to pull myself up onto any of them. The force of the water against building walls caused the pallets to begin stacking on top of themselves. I couldn't get my head above water. There were just too many pallets. The log jam of pallets was too much for me. I was completely submerged and couldn't break through.

I needed to breath, but had no way of getting any air. I pinched my nose with my left hand and covered my mouth with my right hand. I did not want to fill my lungs with this filthy, polluted, black sea water. The urge to breath was becoming relentless. My chest felt as if it was going to burst. And then I didn't remember anything.

I regained consciousness. My left hand was still pinching my nose and my right hand was still covering my mouth. A good thing because when my eyes opened, I was staring at seven yellow-striped fish in front of my face. Looking up, I could see the surface of the water just above my head. In desperate need of oxygen, I burst through it and gasped for air. I stood up. My head and shoulders were above the water. When my lungs were finally satisfied, I wiped water from my eyes and looked around.

I was standing in a small lagoon with the ocean just a short distance away. The ocean was turquoise and blue, but the lagoon was a somewhat dingy brown color. That seemed odd. There was a white sand beach that seemed to curve inward in both directions, suggesting I was on an island. Heading inland beyond the beach were several palm trees and behind the palm trees there looked like a mangrove. There were no hills or mountains to be seen from the beach. The sun was out and there was absolutely no wind. All in all, what a beautiful location.

I trudged out of the lagoon towards the beach and the palm trees. I decided to sit down in a shady spot to figure out where the heck I was and what to do next. As I walked across the beach, there were several fish, starfish, and jellyfish lying dead on the beach. That's weird, I thought. What's the deal with that? I guessed maybe there had been an extreme high tide recently. And the mangrove behind the palm trees looked diseased. Most of the leaves on the ocean-side were brown and dead. Was the ocean spray killing the leaves? Well anyway, having made it to the palm trees I found a log in the shade and sat down.

Taking in the beautiful ocean view, I began to recap what had taken place since I touched the hexagonal crystal plate. I had experienced an earthquake, a tsunami, and now I am here in apparent paradise. None of it makes any sense. Just then the sun went behind a cloud. Somehow, I had missed something back in the Crystals. I hadn't thought about it, but during the earthquake and tsunami, there wasn't the surrounding mist. And looking around there wasn't any mist here, either. It appeared I had no way back to the Crystals or the ETs. I looked up at the palm trees. The fronds were rustling in a breeze coming off the ocean. The breeze began to freshen. It also started to sprinkle. I scanned the area for shelter, but there was none. And the mangrove offered nothing.

The sprinkles turned to rain and then to a pelting downpour. The wind was sending the palm fronds straight out from the tops of the trees. The wind was definitely strengthening. I looked in the direction of where the weather was coming from and saw a dark grey wall of wind and water heading my way; a hurricane! That explained the dead marine life on the beach, the dead leaves in the mangrove, and the muddy waters in the lagoon. I had just been in the eye of this hurricane. And if I remembered correctly, the right side of hurricanes had the most moisture and the strongest winds and it was on its way here.

Since there was no shelter anywhere nearby, I began running down the left side of the beach. It looked like the shortest route to get to the other side of the island and maybe some protection from the wind and the inevitable storm surge. But the sand was too soft for me to make good progress. A gust of wind knocked me down. On all fours, I looked back at the lagoon. Huge waves were rolling over the sand dunes that protected it. Sand was blowing into my eyes despite the pelting rain, making it hard to see. I'd better make my stand here.

I scanned the nearby palm trees. Most of them were too big around, but I saw one that just might work. Trying to keep my balance against the now hurricane-force winds, I managed to walk, then crawl to the palm tree. The diameter of the trunk appeared to be about a foot and a half. I stood behind the tree and put my arms around it locking my fingers together on the other side. The fit was perfect. Not only did I have some protection from the wind, but the tree provided a shield from the blowing sand.

It wasn't the best, but I was feeling pretty good about my chances against the hurricane. I didn't know how long they normally last, but it seemed I could hang on to this palm tree for quite a while. Then I looked around the trunk at the lagoon. The lagoon was gone and the storm surge was heading my way. The height of the storm surge would be dependent on the tide and how much sea water the wind pushed up. To avoid getting swept away, I sat down on the sand and wrapped my legs around the bottom of the tree trunk and overlapped my feet. Having locked my fingers again on the other side of the trunk, I was ready. The incoming water wasn't too bad at first, but soon it was like sitting in a swiftly moving river. The water level was quickly rising. What was waist deep was now at my chest and rising. I decided I'd better start shinnying up the tree to keep my head above water.

The buoyancy of my body in the water made shinnying the first foot up the tree fairly easy. However, the current of the surge was unrelenting and tiring me out. I thought, if I could get up another foot or so, I'd be above the storm surge and could hang on until it passed. So, with all my strength, arm by arm and leg by leg, I managed to go up the trunk about another foot. My legs were still submerged, but I didn't think I was going to be swept away anymore.

Continuing to hang on to the palm tree, my arms and legs began to tire and ache. The storm surge was now up to my waist again. The pain in my arms and legs was getting worse. At this rate, I won't be able to hang on much longer. Wait! I had an idea. If I could turn myself around the tree so my backside was facing the surge and wind, maybe it would be enough to relieve my aching arms and legs.

I began inching my way to the other side of the tree. Each position change on the rough tree bark began to rub the insides of my arms raw and they began to bleed. I had no choice, but to keep at it. Inch by inch I labored at working my way around to the other side. Could my arms and legs hold on until I got all the way to the other side of the tree?

As I kept turning, I began lowering myself in the water. That seemed to speed up my progress. It felt like forever, but finally my back was facing the surge, the wind and the rain. Everything except my head and shoulders was submerged. My arms and legs didn't ache as bad, nor was my body being pushed away from the palm tree by the surge current. Okay, now this might be manageable, I thought. Maybe I can do this; maybe I can survive a hurricane. Just then, a large wave crested over me. I did not see the log that hit the back of my head.

I awoke standing up on a dirt road. Judging by all the grass and weeds in the middle, it wasn't used very often. Looking around, I was in a small valley. The plants and trees were very tropical. Some smaller palm trees dotted the hillsides. The sky was blue with several white clouds and the air was warm and humid. I shook my head; what an idyllic setting. It was beautiful. Just then, there was a massive explosion behind me. The force threw me about eight feet down the road. My head hit the gravel, splitting my forehead open just above my left eye.

The concussion from the explosion impaired my hearing. I couldn't hear anything, but I began to feel the ground shaking intermittently. Rocks, boulders, and stones were showering down all around me. What on earth was going on?! I curled up in a ball as best I could to avoid having my arms and legs getting pummeled by the rocks. One small rock hit my right shoulder. It felt like I had been shot. I reached around with my left hand and pulled the embedded bloody rock from my shoulder. The shower of debris began to subside. Blood was running into my eye making it difficult to see. I sat up and wiped the blood away with my hand. I turned around and looked behind me. A huge plume of ash and dust was being sent skyward from a towering volcano.

As I watched the cloud of ash and dust, something was rushing down the side of the volcano heading into this little valley. It looked like an avalanche, except instead of being white, the avalanche was dark grey. Oh god, a pyroclastic flow, and it's headed right for me! All I knew about pyroclastic flows is that they travel fast and anything that gets in their way of hot toxic gasses and super-heated ash either burns up or melts. I can't waste any more time. I've got to get up and start moving.

I began running ahead of the flow, but also angling up the side of the valley to get to higher ground. Blood is still running in my left eye, making it difficult to see where I was going. I needed both eyes to avoid running into trees, bushes and the debris field of rocks and boulders left by the volcanic explosion. As I ran, I took off my t-shirt, wadded it up and compressed my wound with my left hand; much better. The tropical vegetation was fairly sparse so I could make good time getting to the top of the valley ridge. If I can make it to the top, hopefully it will be high enough to stay above the heat, gas, and ash.

About half way up the ridge I thought I could make better progress if I had both arms pumping. I took the t-shirt off of my forehead. The wound wasn't bleeding as bad as before. With the t-shirt wadded up in my left hand, I began running with both arms free. I was getting closer to the top. My spirits were bolstered. Maybe I can outrun this thing after all. Just then my feet became tangled in some vines and I went down on all fours. I sat up and began fumbling with the vines trying to get my feet untangled. I could feel the air getting hotter and began smelling sulfur. As precious time was being wasted, I finally freed myself. I didn't dare look behind me. I took off running again up the hillside. I had left my t-shirt on the vines.

As I climbed, the plants and bushes thinned out making it easier to run. I estimated I had about fifty feet to the top of the ridge. The muscles in my legs were on fire. I had to drop to my hands and knees and crawl the last twenty feet. The volcanic rocks on the ground were sharp and jagged. The palms of my hands began to bleed. The sharp rocks had cut through the knees of my pants. My knees were now bleeding, too. Finally, I crested the valley ridge. Trying to catch my breath, I turned to see that the flow was traveling down and up the valley's sides. It was becoming hotter and hotter. Was I high enough? I looked for trees or rock formations for higher ground, but there were none. This was it.

With all the dense ash, it was hard to see the flow affecting plants and trees. Then I witnessed a sure sign. My t-shirt burst into flames and immediately disappeared. The surrounding air was getting much hotter and the smell of sulfur gas became overpowering. Then an idea hit me. Maybe I could run down the other side of this ridge. I looked over in that direction. Nope. The flow was on the other side of the ridge, too, and heading up my way to the top. I sat down and curled up. The heat became searing. It felt like my lungs were on fire. I couldn't breathe any more. With my last breath I screamed. Just before I fell unconscious, I could smell burning hair.

I came to, still in the prone position. Jeez, what will it be this time, I thought. First thing, I felt my hair; it was all there. I opened my eyes. My t-shirt was back. I tilted my head up and looked around; corn stalks. Everywhere I looked, there were brilliant green corn stalks. I stood up. The corn stalks were about chest high with some others a little higher. I was in the middle of a huge, flat corn field; field corn as far as the eye could see. Off in the distance was a white, two-story farm house, red barn and silo, with a few out-buildings. Everything looked normal. Maybe I'm back in my own time, who knows? I guess I could make my way to the farm house and figure out how to get home from there.

I started walking in-between the corn rows towards the farm house. It seemed like a nice day, and then some wind came up. A light rain began. As I watched the rain, it became white. Small hail was bouncing off of the corn leaves and me. After a few more steps, the hail was becoming larger and more frequent. And then it was like the skies opened up. The hail was the size of nickels and quarters and the air around me looked completely white. Once again, I crouched in a prone position with my hands over my head. The pain on my hands, neck, and back was excruciating from the pelting hail. I didn't know how long I would be able to put up with this.

After an extremely painful minute or so, the hail began to get smaller and let up some. I stood up. Most of the leaves on the corn stocks were shredded. I looked towards the farm house. It was now getting hammered by the hail. I began my march towards the farm house again. I could hear a faint roaring sound, like distant thunder, but couldn't tell from which direction it was coming. I lengthened my strides. The dull roar was becoming louder and definitely coming from behind me. I turned around and looked. A huge tornado was headed my way.

You've got to be kidding me. Of course, what else would I expect? The tornado's huge funnel was slowly moving from side to side in the corn field. A huge cloud of debris was created where it touched the ground. For a moment, I stood there staring at the tornado watching it twisting through the corn field. I thought, you know, I've survived an earthquake, a tsunami, a hurricane, and a pyroclastic flow. Maybe I could just stand here, let the tornado take me and see where I end up next. I'm really tired of trying to get out of harm's way. I think that's exactly what I'll do. Hmmmm. On the other hand, each time I faced disaster, I tried my best to avoid it. That could be how I had survived so far. I'd better go with the tried and true method. With that thought, I took off running towards the farm house hoping it had a storm shelter.

My route was a zig-zag pattern. I ran for a while between corn rows, then I would cut through the corn rows. This slowed my progress and I couldn't see ahead very well. So after a bit, I switched to running in the corn rows. Over the tops of the stalks, I could see a county road just ahead of me. To the right of the county road was the dirt driveway that led to the farm house. If I could get there I might have a chance. I decided to cut through some more corn rows to make my path to the county road shorter. As I did, I fell five feet down onto a concrete ramp of a loading dock. My hands and arms cushioned the blow to my head, but not my left leg. Something was very wrong. I took one look and knew it was a compound fracture of my femur. The protruding bone made a bulge on the outside of the pant leg. In shock, I thought, now what was I going to do? I looked up the ramp. No, that wasn't an option. Then I looked over to my right and saw concrete steps that lead out of the loading dock ramp. The steps had a metal pipe hand rail. That was going to be my only chance.

Wincing in pain, I dragged myself over to the steps. Using my arms and hands, I positioned myself on the third step. I put my left arm under the rail with my left hand gripping the rail overhead. My right hand went underneath and gripped the rail in front of my left hand. You know, I thought, with some luck the tornado may miss me completely.

The roar of the wind became deafening. Above me, there was debris flying everywhere. I gripped the hand rail as tightly as I could and put my head down in between my arms. Just then, my legs and body were lifted into the air, like I was floating. Feet first, my entire body was vertical. I lost my arm grip on the rail. My hands were the only things keeping me next to the ground. The tornado's wind was just too strong; first my right hand let go, then my left. I flew straight up into the sky. As I rose into the tornado it felt like I was being torn apart, limb by limb. Then blackness surrounded me from all sides.

9

I became aware. This felt different. Raising my eye lids, I went from darkness to blackness. Everywhere was black. It appeared the dark entity had finally captured me. I felt my body; no broken leg and no clothes. I tried to feel for the floor. There wasn't one. Nor were there any walls or ceiling. I was suspended in some kind of black void. Now what? What was going to happen to me? "Is anyone here, or there?" I asked in a strong, loud voice. No answer. That was strange, though. It seemed like my voice was muffled, like it wasn't meant to be heard by anyone, or anything. I tried again; same result. All right, wherever I am, it seems I am alone.

I began thinking about the past few hours. Since the hexagonal crystal plate didn't perform as expected, I was exposed to one natural disaster after another: earthquake, tsunami, hurricane, volcano, and tornado. I was hit in the head by a tree limb, almost drowned, coldcocked by driftwood, hair caught on fire, and then my body being torn apart. The last thing I remembered was being sucked up into the tornado, and then black closing in on me from all sides. And yet, here I was. Somebody or something wanted me alive. At least, I think I was alive.

I worried about Kate. I've been gone way too long. She must be frantic. There was no way of contacting her to let her know that at least I was in one piece. I missed my boys and grandchildren. Will I ever see them again? And if so, when will that be?

I had to go to the bathroom. How was this going to work? Well, I guess I'll just urinate and see what takes place. So, I relieved myself. To my surprise, nothing happened. I didn't short-circuit anything, or stain a carpet, that I know of. The urine just seemed to disappear.

Physically, I seemed fine. Mentally, I was exhausted. From volcanos to tornados, I was just worn out. I'm sure who or whatever has me here will wake me up if it wants to communicate. But I'm going to close my eyes and see if I can fall asleep. And I did.

I was jolted out of a deep sleep. What the hell was that? It sounded like trombones blaring with a mixture of flutes and saxophones. The sound was over-powering. It lasted several seconds. It began loud with a crescendo of several staccatos before it ended. It made no sense. Is something or someone trying to communicate with me? "Is anyone there?" I asked. "I didn't understand what you just said. Can you say all of that over again?"

Silence. Okay, maybe there was something in here with me. I don't know if I felt better or worse knowing I'm probably not alone now. Like it or not, I've got company.

I had fallen asleep again. I dreamt about the old farm house that I grew up in. But particularly, I dreamt about the barn. Growing up, it was the best place to play. The barn always seemed full of hay, cows, smells, and adventures. As kids, we would build forts in the hay, swing on a rope with a gunny sack full of hay tied to it, and spend nights in sleeping bags listening to the wind blow through the plank siding. However, in my dream I was sent to the barn by my mother to tell dad that dinner was going to be ready soon. He was milking the cow. It was winter and at 6:00 in the evening it was very dark outside.

Even in the dark, I knew my way up the hill to the barn and the barn door. I found the handle and opened it. The inside of the barn was dark. The only lightbulb in the barn hung above the stanchions where the milk cow stood. Why hadn't dad turned it on? If dad was in here, he was milking the cow in the dark. I felt for the light switch. It was round and about the size of a tuna can. In the middle of the switch housing was a knob that you twisted to turn the light on. The housing didn't have a cover and every time you twisted the knob, there would be a small spark. I hated that switch. I was always afraid I would get an electrical shock. I turned the knob and heard the familiar click and saw the spark. The light should be on, but it wasn't. I twisted the knob again; nothing. I kept twisting and twisting and twisting...

"WHAT ARE YOU?"

Out of a dream-sleep my head bolts upright by a huge booming voice. I felt like I was going to puke. My mood was suddenly doom and gloom.

"WHAT ARE YOU?"

Shaken, I answered, "I am from earth. I am an earthling".

"IMPOSSIBLE!"

"I can assure you that I am from earth," I exclaimed. Silence. I waited a long time, but no response was forthcoming. We've gone from trombones to English, so some progress had been made. I began thinking that I needed a better answer if the opportunity presented itself again. "I am an earthling" obviously wasn't a satisfactory one. And it seemed I had plenty of time to get my next response ready.

I thought about how long I had been in captivity and isolation. I estimated about twelve to twenty-four hours being in suspension with no food or water. My only measure of time was biological. I have defecated a second time. It's odd, but each time there were no residual effects and absolutely nothing around me. So, was this the master plan to break me, to reveal who I was and what dastardly deeds I had for the Crystals? I kept looking around. I don't know why I did; there was nothing to see. Why is this happening to me? What have I done to deserve this treatment? All I tried to do was help some ETs out. Or did I? Was something else going on here, some other purpose I've become involved with, but don't know anything about? Will I ever see Kate again? And what about Travis, Joel and the grandkids, Jay and Aisa? The more I thought about my situation, the more upset I became about this horrible agreement I had gotten myself into. If I ever get a second chance to communicate with the dark entity, I am going to be relentless in demanding answers and demanding my release from this hell hole. I began to cry. I started screaming obscenities at the dark entity. I began throwing punches and kicking my legs and feet in the black void at everything and nothing. My behavior became increasingly irrational. After what seemed like a long time fighting demons in the dark, I slowly stopped. I was sobbing and couldn't stop. I thought to myself, this whole thing...wait...what's that, a blurry ghost-like shape? I tried wiping the tears from my eyes.

It appeared to be a vertical band of white and blue lights right in front of me. I don't know how far away it was, but it looked to be about six feet long. It was just a band of light. Hold it, something was happening. The band of light was turning on its axis. As it twisted, it had formed a circle consisting of eight white lights evenly spaced around the circumference. In between each white light were eight small blue lights rotating in their own small circle. As I watched, two curved lines came from each side of the circumference with the same circles of blue lights. The whole thing tilted on its north and south axis and became three-dimensional. It resembled a beach ball with six longitude lines with the circles of blue lights on each line. The ball began rotating.

As I was being mesmerized watching this light show, someone put their hand on my right shoulder. My head jerked around to see who was there. My left hand instinctively went to my right shoulder to grab the hand. Nothing. Nothing to see and nothing to feel. Frightened, I turned around to watch the lights again, but they were gone. I was back to blackness, despair, and hopelessness.

I dozed again. When I woke up, I again experienced nausea and foreboding.

"WHAT ARE YOU?"

The booming voice; I was ready this time with my answer. Forcefully, I exclaimed "I am an earthling who agreed to help four Observers retrieve information about their reproduction process. According to them, there had been too many incidents where Observer lives had been lost, and they do not know how to replace themselves. They believe the answers on how they reproduce is within the Crystals. The Observers cannot go in the Crystals. However, with their training, I can. I entered the Crystals to gather this information. Then I was to return to the Observers and present to them what I had discovered!"

Silence. After what seemed several minutes, "Why, those

clever little bastards," was its' response.

With that statement, I felt the tension leave the room.

"What?!" I asked.

"The Observers were never meant for independent thinking," it said.

Still feeling sick to my stomach, I demanded, "What is this all about? Who or what are you?"

After a thoughtful moment, it explained, "Since you put your life in peril for the Observers, I will explain this much. We observe many planets across the galaxy gathering information on how each one evolves. You are the first of any species to actually witness areas of our ongoing activities, hence my concern on what you are and what your purpose of being here is. To answer your second question, I think it best if you do not see or come in contact with me. However, regard me as a librarian."

A librarian?! A librarian. Now that was a disappointment. Still upset, I said, "I've met tougher librarians than you on earth. So how do you guys travel the vast distances of this galaxy?"

Silence.

"Well, what are your purposes in observing the evolution of planets?"

Silence.

"Okay, why was I subjected to an earthquake, tsunami, hurricane, volcano, and tornado before being held captive in some kind of black void?" I demanded.

"Not all crystals are about certain events or people. We do categorize some crystals according to topics. Unfortunately, you touched one categorized by natural disasters. You entered a natural disaster timeZition vortex," was the librarian's explanation.

"All right, I am here to gather information on how the Observers can replenish their population," I said. "Can you please direct me to where I can retrieve this knowledge in the crystal plates?"

"The answer you and they seek is not here," the librarian said.

"What!?" I exclaimed. Dumbfounded, I said, "You mean all of this was for nothing?"

"I am afraid you are correct," said the librarian.

What a huge blow! After everything I had experienced and

endured, I was going home empty handed. Then it occurred to me, "I am going home, aren't I?"

"Yes."

I didn't know what else to say. The librarian was reluctant to answer any questions concerning their huge experiment and findings. No answers or insights about the galaxy seemed forthcoming, either.

Rejected, I asked, "In the vast scheme of things, how are human beings doing?"

There was a pause. Then the librarian explained, "When a species becomes sentient, we apply a simple formula to measure "sustainability" with these three benchmarks: social, environmental, and economical. I will leave you to draw your own conclusions about yourselves."

I didn't know what to say, except, "Thank you." I didn't know if I meant it or not.

Then the librarian said, "Before you return to earth, I am curious and have a question for you. Have you learned anything with all of your experiences concerning the Observers, the earth, the moon, and the Crystals?"

With no hesitation I said, "Yes. Yes, I have." With conviction, I stated, "Everything is connected."

Suddenly, I didn't feel ill anymore and felt very positive about my situation.

"It has been, hmmm, intriguing meeting an observed species. It is time for you to depart."

I found myself standing outside the huge crystal with my hand still on its' surface. I opened my eyes and immediately closed them. I hadn't seen light for probably two days. Even in the dim green glow of the crystals, it hurt my eyes to open them. ~Rosie, everyone, are you still here?~ I thought, ~I can't open my eyes yet, I am not used to the light.~

I was struck with an immense pain in my forehead. I dropped to my knees holding my head with both hands. So this was it, I thought. For failing I am being punished, or worse. And, you know what, I just don't care anymore. To hell with this whole thing, I just don't care. Slowly, the pain subsided. I squinted and looked up. I made out Rosie and saw three shadowy forms in the background. With some effort, I got to my feet. With an unsteady walk, I approached the ETs.

Rosie thought, ~We are sorry. In our excitement, we did not remember that only one of us should communicate with you.~

Excitement?! What was Rosie thinking about? I lowered my eyebrows. ~What excitement?~ I asked. ~I failed. I didn't bring back anything.~ Silence. I felt confusion from the ETs. Finally, Rosie thought, ~You brought back the exact information we needed to begin our reproduction program.~

~What are you thinking about?~ I thought. ~The librarian told me the answers we sought did not lie within the Crystals.~ Then it dawned on me. Somehow the librarian must have given me the information for ET reproduction from its mind to mine without my knowledge. Well, how about that? After all the natural disasters I endured, after being chased by the librarian and held captive for two days, I was successful after all. With a smile on my face, I looked at the ETs and thought, ~Let's go home.~

As we flew over the last mountain and began descending to our front lawn at Pine Creek, I still had a smile on my face. And yet, I know Kate has been just frantic about me being gone for so long. I hope she can find it in her heart to forgive me and the ETs. As Mr. Wizard settled next to our home, I could tell it was early morning. There was a glow in the east, but the sun hadn't risen over the hills yet. I just didn't know which morning it was.

We all gathered on the front lawn. I invited the guys to come into the house. As we approached the front door, Kate came out and greeted us. She gave me a big hug and kiss and said, "I am so relieved you are back here so soon and safe!"

I was confused. I was not getting any of this. "Aren't you frantic that I was gone so long?!" I exclaimed.

"Frantic, why would I be frantic?" Kate asked.

"What day is this?" I asked.

Kate said, "You left at 3:30 this morning. It's the same day."

"What time is it now?" I asked, not really understanding.

"It's 5:30 a.m. I got up early because I couldn't sleep. And then you and the guys just showed up," Kate explained.

I stood there looking at Kate, still confused. By my estimation, I had been gone at least two days. How do these guys do this? Oh, well. With a smile once again on my face, I thought, ~All right everyone, let's go inside and get comfortable.~

Rosie, Lumpy, and James T sat on the brown leather couch while Satchmo inched its' butt back into the La-Z-Boy recliner. I sat in the oak rocker and Kate pulled in a chair from the dining room table. Kate wanted to hear about everything. I explained my first encounter with the librarian, going to the Mojave Desert, the old Ponderosa Pine Estates log home, and then getting caught in a natural disaster timeZition vortex. I described my capture and captivity by the librarian. Kate was fascinated by the prospect of a librarian in charge of the Crystals. I told her about my conversations with it and eventual release. Thinking I had failed, I said I wasn't aware that the librarian had put the Observers reproduction information in my mind.

Then Rosie thought, ~Mike, our association with you has been eventful for us. We have... ~ Rosie paused. You could tell it was searching for the right word to use. Finally, Rosie continued, ~We have enjoyed our time with you and Kate. As you now call our craft Mr. Wizard, it has enjoyed its time with you, too.~

~As an Observer, we have never had an identity,~ Satchmo thought. ~You assigned us designations. We have enjoyed being individuals with different designations.~

Lumpy thought, ~From our very first encounter, our time with you and Kate has elevated our experience of being an Observer.~

And then James T waded in. ~I now know what my designation, James T, means to you. I enjoy being called James T.~

~So James T, is he your favorite captain?~ I asked. No response.

Jeez, this is truly amazing. For the first time, all of them used positive emotional words and descriptions. I don't know what to make of it.

Kate grabbed my hand and squeezed, "They're making me cry."

"Me, too," I answered.

~Rosie, Lumpy, Satchmo, James T,~ I thought. ~It is me who has experienced the greatest human adventure ever. And for that, I am forever grateful to all of you. Thank you so much.~

Following that, the guys stood up and walked out the front door. Kate and I followed. We all assembled under Mr. Wizard. I looked up and thought, ~Mr. Wizard, I had the best time going to Bermuda and returning with you. I hope we can do it again soon.~

~I am in anticipation,~ was the response.

As we stood on the front lawn, Rosie put its hand in my left hand, and Lumpy took my right hand. I looked on either side of me. All of us were standing in a semi-circle holding each other's hands. Kate and the dogs were included with Satchmo and James T putting their hands on the dogs' heads. I don't know the words to Kumbaya, but this was definitely one of those moments. Then, unbelievably, came a rush of pure, positive, loving emotion; warming, soothing, and relaxing. It was the same emotion that I had experienced in the whale's mind and in my own mind. It was so passionate that my legs almost buckled beneath me. I had never experienced this intense positive emotion ever. I turned and looked down at Rosie. His slit was curved in a smile. ~And now, Mike, what can we do for you?~ Rosie asked.

I simply thought, ~Surprise me.~

As they all loaded up into Mr. Wizard, I once again told them not to be strangers. When they were all aboard, the ship turned vertically on its axis and began spinning like a coin flicked by a finger, faster and faster. Then it shot straight up into the morning sky and disappeared.

That evening I was exhausted. Kate and I went to bed earlier than usual. As my head hit the pillow, I began thinking about all of the events of this morning. There were so many. As I thought about them, I could feel sleep coming on fast. I could also smell something. It was like wet dog fur. That's weird, I thought. The dogs sleep in the garage at night. They couldn't be in the house. And yet the smell persisted. Oh well, I'll worry about it tomorrow...zzzz.

Acknowledgements

My grandson, Jaden, says he came up with the black void idea. I don't think so, but it's been over a year since we discussed this book. Remember, I'm old. My memory ain't what it used to be. And he insisted that the Z in timeZition be capitalized. I have no idea why. My granddaughter, Mayan, didn't contribute any ideas or thoughts for the book, but she did shave her head for childhood cancer research while living in Bermuda.

Chris and I have walked the Bermuda Railway Trail many times. Somewhere around Shelly Bay is the signpost with the runaway train story. Except I couldn't remember the story's details nor find it online. But I did find a website about Bermuda history that said it would answer questions about the railroad. So I asked for details about the runaway train, never really expecting an answer. The next day I received an email from Simon Horn. He had written a book about the Bermuda railroad and cordially supplied the details about the runaway train. So when you are in Bermuda, think about buying his book.

Phyllis Emmert, the illustrator, lives just about five houses from ours. In 2020, Phyllis participated in a new artist showing at the Seattle Art Museum. She has art displayed at Confluence Art in Twisp, Washington, and Two Rivers Gallery in Wenatchee, Washington. When I first approached her about illustrating this book, she was extremely enthusiastic about participating in the project. So if you notice, the Sasquatch family have 3 fingers and 3 toes. Is she suggesting something? You will find her paintings and art work at phyllisemmert.com.

My son, Traver, had lived on Bermuda for 15 years and experienced three hurricanes when the eye of the storm went right over the islands. He provided valuable information about hurricane eye conditions. And he asked me, "Do you know the noise you hear the day after a hurricane?" Answer, "Chainsaws."

My youngest son, Jolin, suggested I should be the illegitimate child of one of the ETs. Has he seen these ETs? I don't think it's physically possible to be a legitimate child.

During Covid I wrote a cookbook. It's strictly for family and friends. But I needed someone to publish it. Russel Davis of Gray Dog Press in Spokane, WA, took on my project. He was the best person to work with while I finished the book and sent it off to him. So I visited Russel a few months ago hoping he would publish this book. Gray Dog Press doesn't publish hard-back books, but he agreed to be my liaison to IngramSpark, the publishing company. Thanks Russel.

And last, my lovely wife Chris spent many hours proofreading this book. From misspellings, horrible grammar, and words that didn't make any sense, she corrected them all. But if you find something that should be fixed, blame her.

www.ingramcontent.com/pod-product-compliance
Lightning Source LLC
Chambersburg PA
CBHW060546310726
48982CB00009B/1386/J

* 9 7 9 8 2 1 8 2 9 3 5 0 5 *